...ng for love.
He's search. ,or anything other than love.
Somehow, they might just be each other's best match.

For years Captain Anteros Bourbon—aka *The Cobra*—has eluded his father. He has dedicated his life to fighting the war against Napoleon by building his fleet of ships and sinking his enemy's warships, although he hides a deadly secret. He is a lost Prince of Naples and Sicily, and now his father has found him and is demanding he marry and produce the required heir. Never will he take on a wife though, or expose her to his dangerous activities, so instead he devises a plan to make it appear to his father that he has wed. He enlists the aid of an English lady he trusts by asking her to speak false marriage vows with him. A winning plan for sure, one which should rid him of his father's man spying on him.

Lady Olivia Trentbury has been infatuated with Anteros Bourbon since the first day she met him. He has aided her family in so many ways, and when he arrives on her doorstep asking if she'll speak false marriage vows with him, she can't turn him away. She takes all care when his father's spy is near, although unfortunately the villain is intent on removing her from Anteros's sight. The spy steals her away as his hostage aboard a ship bound for Sicily. Forced to survive treacherous waters as Anteros follows in hard pursuit, she discovers staying alive has never been more of a challenge.

Can Anteros capture his lady back before it's too late?

Books by Joanne Wadsworth

The Matheson Brothers Series
Highlander's Desire, Book One
Highlander's Passion, Book Two
Highlander's Seduction, Book Three
Highlander's Kiss, Book Four
Highlander's Heart, Book Five
Highlander's Sword, Book Six
Highlander's Bride, Book Seven
Highlander's Caress, Book Eight
Highlander's Touch, Book Nine
Highlander's Shifter, Book Ten
Highlander's Claim, Book Eleven
Highlander's Courage, Book Twelve
Highlander's Mermaid, Book Thirteen

Highlander Heat Series
Highlander's Castle, Book One
Highlander's Magic, Book Two
Highlander's Charm, Book Three
Highlander's Guardian, Book Four
Highlander's Faerie, Book Five
Highlander's Champion, Book Six
Highlander's Captive (Short Story)

Billionaire Bodyguards Series
Billionaire Bodyguard Attraction, Book One
Billionaire Bodyguard Boss, Book Two
Billionaire Bodyguard Fling, Book Three

Books by Joanne Wadsworth

Regency Brides Series
The Duke's Bride, Book One
The Earl's Bride, Book Two
The Wartime Bride, Book Three
The Earl's Secret Bride, Book Four
The Prince's Bride, Book Five
Her Pirate Prince, Book Six
Chased by the Corsair, Book Seven

Princesses of Myth Series
Protector, Book One
Warrior, Book Two
Hunter (Short Story - Included in Warrior, Book Two)
Enchanter, Book Three
Healer, Book Four
Chaser, Book Five

The Prince's Bride

Regency Brides, Book Five

JOANNE WADSWORTH

The Prince's Bride
ISBN-13: 978-1-72392-317-3
Copyright © 2018, Joanne Wadsworth
Cover Art by Joanne Wadsworth
First electronic publication: September 2018

Joanne Wadsworth
http://www.joannewadsworth.com

AUTHOR'S NOTE:
This book is a work of fiction. The names, characters, places, and incidents are products of the writer's imagination or have been used fictitiously and are not to be construed as real. Any resemblance to persons, living or dead, actual events, locale or organizations is entirely coincidental. The author does not have any control over and does not assume any responsibility for third-party websites or their content.

Published in the United States of America

First digital publication: September 2018
First print publication: September 2018

To Be, or Not to Be, That Is the Question.

The British Museum, a year and a half earlier...

Lady Olivia Trentbury rested one hand on the edge of the carriage window as the horses trotted up the promenade to the grand entrance of Montagu House. The coach swept around to the front and halted before the British Museum's stately main entrance, the building rising two stories high with a protruding mansard roof. The patchy gray sky overhead didn't deter her from alighting down the steps and onto the gravel driveway. No, not when she had an important meeting to attend, or she should say an important rendezvous with the most mysterious man she'd ever met.

A light misty rain fell and with her parasol raised, she hurried across the forecourt and inside the front door, her maid falling in behind her. Usually the sheer beauty of the paintings and exhibits had her enthralled for hours, but not today. Her mysterious man beckoned.

Following the curves of the wide winding staircase rising around the perimeter of the central saloon, she ascended to the second floor. She whisked through double doorways framed by elegant arches, passed several well-crafted displays where visitors stood in groups admiring the exhibits, then hurried onward. So many upper rooms.

Once she reached the far recesses of the museum and entered a shadowy corridor lined with a series of dusty marble statues, she slowed her pace and halted before a heavy wooden-paneled door. From her reticule swaying over her arm, she removed the missive Captain Anteros Bourbon had sent her and pressed it against the ruffled front of her long-sleeved lavender walking dress.

"Are you certain you wish to go in, my lady?" Concern clouded her maid's eyes as the young woman waited behind her.

"Very certain." She passed her reticule and parasol to Lucy. "Wait here for me."

A dip of her maid's head, her frilly white bonnet bobbing.

"She'll be safe with the captain." Giovani stepped out from the shadows and tipped his hat, his dark Italian looks making her maid squeak.

"Do not fear Giovani. He would never hurt either of us." She squeezed her maid's hand then stepped up to Giovani with a heartfelt smile. "Good morning. How is the captain this day?"

"Lady Olivia, *piacere*. It is always a pleasure to see you. The captain is well." A suave catch of her gloved fingers, a kiss pressed to her knuckles and a scandalous wink too. Not unusual for the captain's right-hand man. "It appears you received his letter last night," Giovani murmured in a low drawl.

"Yes." She cleared her throat. She'd gotten quite the shock when she'd retired to bed for the night and discovered the missive tucked underneath her pillow. "Did, ah, the captain deliver it himself?"

"*Sì*, of course." A sinful smile as he eased back into the shadows. "Go and see him, my lady. The captain misses his *angelo*."

"I shall, but make sure you don't scare my maid again." She opened the door and without any further hesitation, stepped inside the room which the captain had chosen for their meeting. A window allowed a touch of daylight in, dust motes catching in the muted rays, the specks swirling as she closed the door behind her. In the center of the room stood a large lifelike sculpture of Anteros, the Greek god of love and passion. Wings sprouted from the statue's back, while a cloth lay draped for modesty over the sculpture's shoulder and around his lower body, his chest exposed and muscles flexed as he held a bow with an arrow on the verge of being released. She wandered across to the beautiful piece, touched a finger to the statue's curves and—

The captain's chest brushed against her back, one of his hands discreetly settling on her hip. In her ear, he whispered, "You give your trust so easily, *il mio bellissimo angelo*."

My beautiful angel. She loved it when he called her that.

"I give my trust to those who deserve it." Swishing away, she carried on around the statue, her lavender skirts brushing the polished floorboards, the engraved locket at her neck swaying against the ruffled bodice of her gown. "Why have you called for this meeting, sir?"

"Straight to the point, as always." He followed her, his black riding breeches tucked into knee-length boots polished to a high sheen, his hat shading the top half of his silky black hair, the collar of his superfine jacket sitting high and hiding the lower half of his face. He stopped in front of her, lifted the locket at her neck and slowly rubbed his thumb along the engraving of *the cobra*. "Why did you have my insignia etched upon your locket?"

"Your diamond earring is locked away inside this charm for safe keeping." When she'd passed by the jeweler's shop in town a week ago, it had seemed only right to request the locket housing his jewel be inscribed with his mark. That of the cobra, a venomous snake that could strike if others ever dared to enter its territory. Much like the man himself. He protected those he considered his, a category she'd now fallen into.

"I had Giovani give you my diamond earring so you knew the message he conveyed came directly from me." Husky words, his gaze locked with hers. "At the time I was chasing a killer and couldn't speak to you in person, the mission too dangerous."

"You've now completed that mission." A mission she was aware of since it had involved the captain keeping her sister and brother-in-law alive. Not wanting to return his diamond but knowing she should, she wet her lips and forced herself to ask the next question. "Would you like your diamond earring back?"

"Do you truly wish to return it?" His gaze softened, although the chiseled line of his jaw remained strong and firm. "Be honest with me."

"Honestly, no."

"Then you must keep it, and I will always know where to find it, adorning the neck of my *angelo*." He went quiet, remaining silent for a long minute or two, the shadows in the room somehow clinging to him even though he stood directly before her in the muted light. "Why is it that you aren't scared of *the cobra*?"

"If you mean you, then I'll never be frightened of being in your presence. You make me feel safe, guarded and protected. You are the last person in the world who would ever hurt me."

"You are one of the few people who do not fear me."

"Well, I have seen who you truly are. Underneath your fierce and secretive countenance is a man who cares for those he is drawn to protect. I like him, very much."

"We are opposites, you and I. Where I am fierce, you are gentle. Where I am secretive, you are completely open." A soft caress of his finger over the engraving. "*La tua bellezza risplende.*"

"Pardon?" She always melted inside when he spoke Italian, or any of the other several languages she'd heard him utter. He spoke several languages with fluent ease, often intermingling Italian and Portuguese, Spanish and Sicilian.

"Your beauty shines forth." Another rub over the engraving, his voice so deep and sultry as it rumbled around her. "So says *the cobra*."

"Why have you called for this meeting, Captain?"

"Anteros."

"My apologies. Anteros."

"*Desidero più tempo con te.*" A wicked smile.

More Italian. It seemed he enjoyed remaining elusive, always slightly out of her reach, but his sapphire eyes emitted a heat that constantly unhinged her. He was even more handsome than Giovani, more darker, more powerfully strong, more of everything. "Which means what, pray tell?"

"I desire more time with you." He stared at her mouth, his gaze going heavy, which made heat curl in her middle.

"You are a terrible flirt." Which she tried to say with a scolding tone, but instead came out in a breathy whisper.

"You said you liked me, very much." He removed his hat and tucked it under one arm, ran a hand through his midnight-black hair, the length sweeping his shoulders, the ends shimmering a vibrant blue, the exact same shade as his magnificent eyes.

"In the way of friendship." Since this man had saved the lives of her loved ones, she owed him a great debt, one she intended on personally repaying. Perhaps that day had now arrived. "Is something wrong? Do you need my aid for some reason?"

"No, nothing is wrong." He sauntered toward the window and leaned one shoulder against the polished wooden frame, his gaze on the extensive rear gardens beyond where visitors to the museum could wander about at their leisure. "I'm leaving for a while." A sad, reflective tone.

"How long? Tucking his missive away in her pocket, she moved slowly toward him and gently touched his arm.

"I will miss you, *mio angelo*." He continued to stare out the window.

"How long?"

"Three months."

"Where are you going?"

"I have renewed my current contract with your English king and the Portuguese royal family. My entire fleet of warships are authorized to capture all merchant ships of French origin currently sailing into English or Portuguese waters along the seaward trade routes. I shall be blocking as much movement as possible made by Napoleon's navy. I can't allow the French to sneak past England's defenses via the coastline."

"Does that mean Adrestia will be leaving soon too?" His sister had become a close friend of hers this past month, a young woman who captained one of her brother's vessels.

"My sister will be sailing *The Decadence*. I'll be sailing *The Cobra*. We work best when we're together." He faced her, his gaze narrowing. "I wished to speak to you about a personal matter before I left. I have delved deeper into Baron Herbarth's personal situation."

Surprised and shocked, her mouth fell open. "I, why would you do such a thing?"

"Herbarth wishes to marry a lady who comes with a large dowry, just as you do."

"The baron and I are friends, the same as you and I are, that is all." She had only recently turned two and twenty, although her eldest brother, Winterly, would expect her to marry soon now that both her elder sisters had wed.

"You must take care around the Earl of Haverlocky too. This past year he has gambled a veritable fortune away and is now searching for more funds."

"He is naught more than an acquaintance. Do not worry yourself over Lord Haverlocky." The captain certainly knew how to source information for those who paid him well for it, which she wouldn't put past her brother in having instigated. "Did Winterly hire you to uncover this information?"

"No, of course not." He stuck his hat back on his head, tugged on the lapels of his jacket. "Do you believe in seers?"

"I've, ah, never had the pleasure of meeting one. Why the change in subject?"

"A seer once told me that you and I are destined to continually cross paths. Shira Ria is a wise old woman, an interfering one too." A lift of his lips, his smile evidence he cared greatly for the seer. "Sometimes she states all sorts of strange things, but her words always ring true." He cupped one of her cheeks, softly stroked his fingers back and forth. "I shall always be here to warn you away from any other men seeking to use you for their own gain. You and my sister have forged a strong friendship, while you and I have too. I guard and protect those I consider family."

"I consider that an honor." Unable to help herself, she rubbed her cheek into his palm. "I'll miss you too, Anteros."

"When I return, I shall come and see you."

"Stay safe out on the water."

"I always do." He dipped in, kissed her forehead, then swept out the door.

He was gone. For three long months.

Her heart panged.

Chapter 1

The Bay of Algiers, Algiers, on board The Cobra, late 1811, eighteen months later...

Captain Anteros Bourbon lowered his skiff over the side of his ship anchored in the night-shrouded waters of the Bay of Algiers. With his back to the coastline, he slipped his oars into the water and heaved, a black headdress veiling his face and a black robe covering his body. "I don't want word spreading to my father that I'm here."

"Provided we remain clear of your father's spies, all should be well." Giovani, his right-hand man, kept his gaze on the shoreline, his body robed and face covered just as his was, the night air hanging heavy and sticky with the heat of the desert flowing from the distant orange sandhills beyond the citadel.

"With all this unrest due to Napoleon, everyone is on edge. Father even more so." Over his shoulder, lights glittered on land and he adjusted his direction with an extra turn of one oar. On course again, his destination the eastern end of the citadel's fortified walls, he guided them toward land. This night, he would be visiting the seer, Shira Ria. Her wise counsel was needed during the immense unrest currently plaguing him. Thankfully, his ship where it remained at anchor, had now disappeared into the dark, which meant what he could no longer see, so too could no one else from the shore.

As the hull of the skiff scraped the sandy curve of the bay, he set the oars inside then splashed over the side into the knee-deep waters, Giovani bounding out on the other side.

Together, they gripped the bow and hauled it half up onto the shore.

Sliding his saber free, he snuck up the beach toward the outer wall which surrounded the city, his man at his side. The wall was built of stone and supported by arches, with a succession of cannons running the entire curved length of the city, the firepower used against those who might try to attack in the hope of taking the citadel for themselves. This stronghold sat at the edge of the desert, the Kasbah of Algiers emitting immense power under the governing rule of the almighty Dey. This city was a haven and a fortress holding mystery and sway, where the dark of night governed over the light of day, yet also a place where immense beauty could enchant the eye of the beholder.

Taking the covert route very few knew about, he and Giovani moved silently around the wall, then they dug their boots in deep as they climbed the sandy hill toward a secret gap in the stonework. No guard. Perfect. He stole inside, plastered himself to the inner wall, he and Giovani remaining shadows as they swept around the perimeter.

They ran in some places, ducked and dived about in others, then once they reached the main square of the marketplace where closed stalls and brightly colored tents were erected, he drew in the faint scent of the rich and spicy scents which still lingered from during the day.

As a boy, he'd visited this square often and reveled in the swarm of people and the bustling energy of the place. Treasures from around the east packed the marketplace, right alongside stolen goods from the west. Stall vendors would haggle with loud shouts and enticing offers, the merchants incredibly crude yet also transfixing to watch as they sought to sell their wares.

Near one closed stall, a parrot in a cage shrieked. Not helpful. Quickly, he scooped a forgotten slice of apple from the cobbles and tossed it to the bird to keep it quiet. The bird gobbled the treat while they rushed past.

He and Giovani continued through the city, then down a street where houses stood wall to wall in a mix of decorative pastel colors. Only one house beckoned him this night, the home belonging to Shira. Within the dark, he stole up to her red door and swiftly rapped as the gentle flutter of washing on the rope strung across the balconies overhead blew in the breeze.

Shira's door creaked open and the seer appeared with a beaming smile, her wise eyes filled with unshed tears. With a whispered breath, she bade them inside, "Come in, come in, my *emir*. You mustn't linger outside, not when your father's spies constantly roam the streets."

"We've taken great care thus far." He stepped into the

warmth of Shira's home, Giovani closing the door behind them. After sweeping his headdress off, he grasped Shira's warm and wrinkled hand then kissed her knuckles. "Peace be unto you, Shira."

"*As-salamu alaykum,* my beloved boy." She cupped his cheeks. "I have missed you."

"As I have missed you." He drew Shira into his arms, his next words heavy with emotion, "It has been far too long since my last visit. I apologize profusely."

"I *saw* you would soon arrive and have waited up for you this night." Shira squeezed him back, her bones frail but her hold incredibly tight. "You have brought Giovani with you, correct?"

"He certainly has." Giovani removed his headdress and offered her a gallant bow. "*Marhaba*, Shira."

"*Marhaba*, Giovani. Come and sit." She released an excited murmur as she drew them both into her small blue parlor. "Knowing you would wish to have your fortunes read, I have already brewed one of my special coffees."

"You know us too well." He and Giovani eased down onto the low pillows spread around a short table where an oil lamp glowed underneath an earthenware dish propped on a wireframe above it. The heavenly scent of oriental spices wafted free, along with the rich fragrance of Shira's special coffee from a coffee pot sitting to one side.

"Wait here. I have prepared food for you as well. You must eat with me." Shira bustled off to her kitchen in the next room and soon returned with a tray holding three cups and a platter of cooked flatbread, stuffed dates, and dried fruits. She set the dishes down and served them each a cup of coffee before taking her own seat on a red and blue embroidered pillow across from them, her legs crossed. "Tell me, Anteros, what has been happening with you since your last visit. I am eager to hear more about your English lady."

"She is currently being pursued by a suitor I don't approve of." Lord Haverlocky no longer chased after her, not when he'd paid a visit to the man and they now had an understanding, but Lord Herbarth was a different matter. The baron had managed to gain Olivia's sympathy following the recent death of his mother. Three proposals she'd received from the baron so far, each one she'd thankfully turned down, but each proposal had only infuriated him more.

"In your eyes, no one will ever be good enough for her." A knowing nod from Shira, the silver and gold bangles adorning her wrists jangling. "You should bring her to see me. In fact, I insist you do."

"I can't steal her away from England just so the two of you can meet." Yet pure longing to do exactly that rushed forth.

"She is in need of a grand adventure, one only you can provide. Bring her to me as soon as you are able." Shira sliced thin curls of cheese from a block of cheese and spread them over the warm flatbread, the cheese quickly melting into a gooey mess his mouth watered to taste.

"Ahh, Shira, I have surely missed your cooking." Since there was no arguing with Shira, he instead helped himself to the savory flatbread. He moaned around a mouthful, the delicious and spicy flavors bouncing off his tongue.

"Eat as much as you please." She beamed like a proud

mother. "I don't wish to see any of the food I've prepared this night to go to waste, and I can only eat so much." She bustled away, then returned with a plate of nuts roasted in honey and dark carob powder. "Try some of these too. I made them especially for you and Giovani."

Shira never prepared anything without great thought as to what she believed was needed for her guests. He scooped a handful of nuts and tossed them back. The texture and taste of the carob powder sprinkled on top zinged off his tongue, the rich sweetness of the carob the perfect balance against the saltiness of the nuts.

A kiss of his fingers in appreciation. "*Delizioso,* Shira. For what reason did you make these?"

"Carob heightens and boosts a man's fertility." He spluttered and Shira giggled like a little girl. "It will not hurt you and Giovani to increase the potency of your seed, yes?"

"I'm certain it will hurt since I don't intend on fathering any children." He pushed the platter of nuts closer to Giovani. "You need these far more than I do."

"*Sì,* give them all to me. I want a wife who will give me plenty of *bambini.*" Giovani scooped the nuts and chewed with a grin.

"Come now, finish your coffee," Shira advised. "It is time I read your fortune again, you too, Giovani. Who wishes to go first?"

"Giovani will." Anteros needed another moment to calm himself after Shira's declaration.

"Help me find the right woman, Shira." Giovani passed his empty cup of coffee to Shira. "If you see any sign of her, you must tell me."

"Let me see." Shira spilled the remains of Giovani's coffee onto a saucer and studied the markings she saw, her azure eyes glowing as she lifted her gaze to his man. "Giovani, you need to pay heed to my words. On the eve of the new year to come, the time will finally be right for you to embark on a journey across the seas with a woman who will unfortunately test your patience. Follow your heart. That is my advice. For if you do, she will be the right woman for you, the one who brings you great joy."

"May I ask her name?" Giovani leaned closer, his curiosity clear to see.

"That I can't disclose, not today, although she is your north star, your guiding light and will radiate warmth and compassion, intrigue and adventure too. Always keep her in your sight."

"I shall do so." Giovani squeezed Shira's hand. "Thank you for your generous words of wisdom."

"You are most welcome." Shira turned to him and held out her hand for his cup. "Your turn, Anteros."

"Be gentle with me." He placed his cup in her hands. "No more talk of boosting my fertility."

"We shall see." She tipped the remains of his coffee onto his saucer and tapped her chin as she concentrated on the residual pattern before her. With her brow wrinkling, she lifted her gaze back to his. "Hmm, this is interesting. I see that you must set sail this very night and travel north. I'm afraid it's about your father. You will meet him on the morrow, and when you do, you must be prepared to listen to him. He will insist on a change, altering your current course on a new pathway. If you do as he says, heartache will soon be yours. Instead, follow your instincts and your heart."

"What will my instincts and heart say?"

"That your angel is the only one to aid you in your coming plight. Allow her to spread her wings and fly, then you too shall see her strengths arise."

"I don't want to involve Olivia in my life, or at least not any more than I've already done."

"You were never meant to live a solitary existence, Anteros. Don't allow the relationship you've seen between your parents to influence your future." Shira pinned him with a determined look. "There are even more dangerous days coming for you, a time in which you must trust in what I've said. Your angel will soon be both the intervention and the prevention of your death. Keep her at your side, day and night, whether you are on her English soil or sailing the dangerous waters you know so well."

"You ask too much of me, Shira."

"No, it's time for you to leave the dark behind and enter into the light. All I ask is that you accept your new future and allow it to flow into complete alignment with your angel's. You'll never regret doing so, provided you cleave unto her, embracing all that you can be together."

An impossible request. Damned impossible.

Chapter 2

Holding the fur hood of her black cloak in place about her face, Olivia hurried along the sidewalk with her maid only a few steps behind. The wind pulled at the emerald skirts of her day gown, darkness closing in as night fell. Up ahead, her driver opened the door of the coach and she picked up her pace and climbed inside. "Thank you, Haroldson."

"Home now, my lady?" Haroldson flicked up the collar of his thick black coat, his nose a bright red from the biting cold.

"Not yet, I'm afraid. I have one more call to make. Take me to Captain Bourbon's place of business. I need to check on Wills. The boy has been so lonely of late." She'd become so fond of Wills, a lad who the captain considered family. He'd rescued Wills from men who'd sought to hurt him, then taken the boy under his wing. She settled herself against the plush burgundy squabs of the coach, while Lucy took the seat across from her. She was ever so grateful

Mama and Winterly had no issue with her paying a call on the boy.

Haroldson closed the door and the coach rocked as he took his seat atop the conveyance.

The coach jerked forward and they bumped along the street. She set her reticule on the seat beside her, removed her kid gloves and rubbed her chilled fingers together. Once a little warmer, the brazier at her feet emitting a lovely heat too, she touched her locket and gently stroked the cobra insignia.

Out her window, vendors stood next to their carts as they hawked their wares, the late hour not worrying them. Two boys with caps on their heads and soot smeared across their cheeks dashed along the sidewalk, likely racing each other to get home before it got too dark.

A rumble of thunder shook the ground and lightning slashed the skies. They would be in for some nasty weather this night. She wiped the fog from her window and searched through the darkness. They passed alongside the murky brown waters of the Thames, this stretch of the river holding hundreds of ships at berth. Wooden walkways were illuminated here and there by the odd street lamp. Dockworkers with thick woolen coats hurriedly pushed wheeled trolleys loaded with supplies into adjacent warehouses.

A few more turns along the cobbled streets and they left the docks behind before entering into an exclusive area. Captain Bourbon's club and public dining rooms held a curiously enviable position in London, what with his business being tucked away on a street not far from the busyness of the docks, yet also rather close to the elegant wealth of Mayfair. Patrons of his exclusive club could enjoy the main saloon and the gaming on offer, while other members from Society who didn't wish to gamble could make use of the public dining rooms and enjoy a meal.

Only a year and a half ago his club had held a far darker image, but things had changed once he'd decided to alter the rules of his club and the patronage he allowed. Even ladies could now gain a membership, provided they too abided by the rules of the house. Of course, only a handful of married ladies had in fact procured said membership, while at least a dozen miffed gentlemen had turned up their noses at the change and swiftly left.

Haroldson slowed the carriage as they arrived at their destination, the stone building beyond her window holding a Palladian façade with French motifs and a gray slate roof. Once the conveyance rocked to a halt, her driver bounded down and set the steps in place before holding a brolly and covering her head from the misty rain as she alighted to the ground. A tug of her gloves back on and she stepped forward. Near the front door of the building, a stylish sign swung on iron clasps, the board showing a golden cobra with its head high and body coiled tight, the serpent hissing over top of a sapphire-colored backdrop. The same insignia on her locket.

Directly next door to the gaming club stood the captain's personal residence, candlelight shining from a window or two along the second floor. She spotted Bellini, the captain's elderly butler, bustling past one window as he closed the drapes for the night. Anteros wasn't due home from sea for another two weeks, but Adrestia should be arriving in port in the next few days since she'd set sail on a separate mission to her brother. She couldn't wait to see Adrestia and to hear all about her recent travels.

With her driver shielding her and Lucy against the worst of the drizzle, she climbed the steps of the club so she could enter the area which opened up to the public dining room. Haroldson lifted the brass knocker and rapped.

The door swung open and the manager swept forward, the burly man dressed in impeccably pressed attire, his jacket and breeches a deep shade of gray with a strip of white edging the cuffs of his sleeves and the lapels of his jacket. He gave her a short bow. "Good evening, Lady Olivia."

"Good evening to you too, Mr. Hodges."

"I take it you're here to see Wills? The boy is barely keeping out of trouble today. Do come in. It's far too cold outside tonight." He took a few steps back and gestured for her to enter. "May I take your cloak?"

"Yes, thank you." She loosened the ties at her neck and handed him the black fur-lined garment. "Where will I find our favorite troublemaker?"

"The dining room. He's sweeping up after he knocked a potted plant over."

"Did the plant survive the fall?"

"Barely. Oh, and before you seek him out, I should tell you that Miss Adrestia Bourbon has returned from sea and is in residence next door."

"Are you absolutely certain?" Adrestia always sent word immediately when she sailed into port. "I haven't heard from her."

"She only arrived an hour ago. Would you like me to

send a message to Bellini? Miss Bourbon will scold me if she discovers you're here to see Wills and I haven't informed her." A pointed lift of his chin, one that said he didn't wish for that to occur.

"Yes, please send her a message. I wouldn't want to be the cause of a scolding."

"Excellent." Mr. Hodges flicked a finger toward one of the uniformed footmen and passed the man her cloak. "Hang this in the cloakroom, then step next door and ask Bellini to inform his mistress of Lady Olivia's arrival. She'll be in the main dining room with Wills."

"Right away, sir." The uniformed footman left, her cloak draped over one arm as he hurried down the redwood paneled passageway to the cloakroom.

"Would your maid like a cup of tea while she waits for you?" Mr. Hodges asked with a glance at Lucy.

"Yes, that would be lovely." She touched Lucy's arm. "Wait for me in the foyer."

"Yes, my lady." Lucy swept across to the foyer in her serviceable gray woolen skirts to the alcove where a group of chairs sat, the main gaming hall just beyond the foyer currently screened by several well-placed palms that reached high to the ceiling.

Olivia left Hodges and walked through the arched doorway into the hallway leading to the public dining room. From under her chin, she untied the silk ties of her emerald bonnet, slid it free and tucked a few loose strands of her golden hair, which had escaped her chignon, behind her ear. She slowed as she passed a row of painted landscapes, just as she did each time she wandered along this passageway.

The first painting showcased a ninety-gun frigate riding the high swells of a stormy sea, the captain's gold and sapphire-colored cobra banner flying proud from the top of *The Cobra's* mizzenmast, the ship named after its master.

On the upper deck at the wheel stood Anteros himself, his midnight-black hair blowing about his shoulders and the wind plastering his white tunic against his broad chest. He wore no cravat or waistcoat, the ties of his tunic whisking about and exposing the deep V of his skin. He appeared like the rogue gentleman he was, giving no care to conforming to Society's rules. He walked his own path, choosing his own way, living his own life as he deemed fit. A rare man indeed. Very few gentlemen she knew opposed the standard convention expected of them the way he did.

A quick look both sides of the passageway to check she remained alone. With a slightly shaky hand, she lifted one finger and trailed down the molded strength of his strong legs covered in tight-fitting black breeches, the glinting length of his saber strapped at his hip blending in with the gold stripe down the side. With his booted feet planted wide on the deck and his powerful arms gripping the wheel, he kept his ship on course over the tumultuous rise of the waves.

She released a dreamy sigh, her heartbeat fluttering, her hand falling back to her side.

Anteros had always fascinated her. She'd never forget the elaborate masked ball she'd attended a little over a year and a half ago at Frederick House, only a few days after she'd first met him. He'd arrived attired head to toe in black with no other adornment save for the large diamond which twinkled from his right ear. His black satin mask had concealed his expression, making him ooze mystery with his hair slicked back and his blue eyes shining as deep and as bottomless as rich sapphires. He'd appeared dark and dangerous behind his mask, a man one didn't trifle with unless they enjoyed said danger.

She'd been completely and irrevocably intrigued.

With no one still in sight, she released the clasp of her locket and tipped the diamond earring within it into her palm. The gold ear hook glittered, the jewel adorning it catching the candlelight from the overhead lantern and sprinkling prisms of gold and white over the wall.

Memories surged from that night long ago when she'd first seen this earring dangling from his ear.

In the ballroom of Frederick House, Anteros had caught her gloved hand and kissed her fingertips, his blue gaze searing into hers, his words a soft murmur as he'd greeted her, "Un bellissimo angelo. You look radiant tonight."

"Captain." A soft sigh had escaped her lips before she'd promptly tugged her hand back. "My papa once warned me that when a man lavishes such words of praise on a lady, that she should take immense care around him. You seem to be a dangerous puzzle I can't quite work out."

"Your papa was clearly a wise man." His lips had tugged up into a sinful grin. "Might I add my own words of warning to his?"

"Go right ahead."

"When a man collects enemies at every turn, just as I have a habit of unfortunately doing, you should steer clear of that man. Immense care must be taken."

"*I, ah—*" *She hadn't known where to look in that moment, his brutal honesty enlightening.* "*Your warning has been duly noted.*" *Not that she'd paid any attention to that warning over the next year and a half to come.*

"*Good evening, Lady Olivia.*" *A masked gentleman had whisked across the ballroom and picked up her dance card. He'd swiftly signed his name alongside the next two dances. Baron Herbarth. Only he had ever attempted to commandeer her dance card at every ball she attended.*

"*Lord Herbarth, how did you know it was me?*" *Her voice had been pitched a little too high, her mask clearly not hiding her identity as it should have.* "*Goodness, reserving two dances with a lady on one night will cause a stir and my mama will end up having words with me. I'm certain we've spoken of this before.*"

"*Yes, we have, but hopefully your mama will speak only wonderful words.*" *The baron had chuckled as he'd eyed her, while Anteros had growled under his breath at the interruption.* "*Surely, Lady Olivia, you can't fault me for wishing to dance with such a delightful companion. I'm certain you'll be inundated with gentlemen and I didn't wish to miss out.*"

Another low growl from the captain, his sapphire eyes hardening to a deeply black hue.

"*You collect enemies, remember?*" *She'd pressed a hand to Anteros's arm to calm him, then faced Herbarth.* "*Lord Herbarth, I believe you are right, and I shall concede to two dances.*"

She'd left Anteros behind and indeed danced with the baron that night, all while knowing how deviously she'd been tugging on the tail of *the cobra*, the first time of many times to come.

Carefully, she slotted Anteros's diamond away and closed her locket.

She continued on down the passageway and when she reached the dark elegance of the dining room, she stepped through the wide double doorway and searched for Wills. Highly polished tables graced the main area with gentlemen seated in their silk waistcoats and tailed coats enjoying a meal. Four ladies in richly-colored gowns and lacy shawls sat amongst the fifty or so men, respectable ladies from within the *ton*. Adrestia had told her that the gentlemen were far less reckless when their wives joined them in the main saloon, and the ladies also enjoyed the exciting atmosphere.

Once, when she'd left Lucy in the foyer before making her way to the dining room, she'd even spotted Lady Wentfall and her widowed sister playing at the whist tables, two ladies who'd in the past been lamenting the downfall of the gaming clubs and who now saw the enjoyment that could be had instead.

Wait staff moved about the tables—gas lamps radiating warmth from the wall sconces and corner stands—while the hearty aroma of exquisite food wafted through the air. The dinner menu here now surpassed that which could be found anywhere else in town, the menu consisting of venison pie, honey-roasted partridge, baked salmon, pigeons in white sauce, and smoked trout, along with seasoned potatoes and roasted vegetables. The chef and his culinary team made the most delicious cakes, pastries, treats, and other masterful delicacies too.

One time the chef had even presented her and Adrestia

with a baked custard dish, the creamy custard cooled and sitting between layers of sweet flaky pastry, the dish topped with thickened cream and a spill of fresh raspberries. Her mouth watered just at the memory of it.

"G'day, my lady." Wills suddenly appeared, skipped in a circle around her before coming back in front and offering her a tip of his cap. His mop of brown hair slid forward as he did, the length hiding his eyes until he pushed the strands back. A streak of dirt smeared one cheek and his nose, while a bit of greenery stuck out from behind his ear. In tan breeches and suspenders, his dark brown woolen jacket slightly too large for his thin frame, he beamed. "The cap'n isn't back yet, but Miss Adrestia is at home. She sailed into port this evenin'."

"Mr. Hodges has sent word to her that I'm here." She plucked the greenery from behind his ear and dropped it into his hand. "How have you been this week?"

"I'm gettin' a tutor, or so Miss Adrestia says." The boy bounced around her, grinning and beaming as he waved the greenery like a flag. "She says I need to learn my letters and to speak all proper like she do—does—nay, do. Ugh." He wrinkled his nose, hands slapping his sides. "Which word is the right one?"

"Does is correct." She tapped the tip of his nose. "It'll be wonderful for you to have a tutor. It's important to gain an education. It'll afford you more opportunities in the future with regard to employment."

"As long as the tutor teaches me how to read sailin' charts along with my letters, then I can help the cap'n and mayhap learn how to sail my own ship one day, just like 'im."

"Him."

"That's what I said." He scrunched one side of his face as if thinking through his answer. "Oh, him."

"That's better." She giggled. "You are a delight, Wills."

"The cap'n calls me his *mascalzone*." Wonder filled his eyes. "I'm not sure what that means, 'cept he says it with a wink, so 'tis likely good."

"It means rascal." Adrestia breezed in wearing a white ruffled blouse and azure blue skirts, a white and blue braided belt at her waist and the tasseled ends sweeping down to her knees. With her midnight-black hair swishing in long glossy curls down her back, she straightened one of Wills' suspenders and said to the boy, "Ask one of the waiters to bring me and Lady Olivia a pot of tea and two custard pastries. I've been dreaming of them while I've been at sea."

"Right away." The boy skipped off toward the waiter across the far side of the dining room.

Adrestia swept up and squeezed her tight. "My sweet friend, I've missed you terribly."

"I've missed you too. Welcome home." She squeezed Adrestia back. "You must tell me all about your trip."

"I visited Lisbon and left supplies there, then stopped off and saw friends here and there on my return."

"What is Lisbon like?" The seaside city sat at the very southern tip of Portugal. Her brother, Harry, had spent time there during the war. He and his fellow soldiers from the 18th Royal Hussars had been based at St. Vincent's Fort, the English soldiers aiding the Portuguese people in protecting the city of Lisbon from Napoleon's advancement.

"The port is filled with rowdy sailors and taverns galore." Adrestia drew her toward the quietest corner and they sat at a table partially hidden from view by a hand-painted oriental screen.

"You must share more than that, particularly since I live vicariously through you. Which is your favorite country to visit?"

"Hmm." A tap of her chin, a sparkle in her eyes. "I adore the beauty of the Maghreb Coastline where the Arabian influence is strong. Then there are the whitewashed buildings and vast desert sands of Algiers— so stunning. But so too are the Sicilian temples which are a treasure to roam. Naples is infused with its own beauty and charm and I always spend time there when passing through." The sparkle in her eyes brightened. "The people of Naples now call me *sorella del cobra*, sister of *the cobra*. I adore that they do."

"Your brother has quite the reputation on the high seas, doesn't he?"

"He isn't known as *the cobra* for no reason. No one wishes to have him on their tail." Adrestia leaned across and caught her hand. "You've never been scared of him though. He calls you his *angelo*."

"He has never given me any reason to fear him."

"He never will either. You are precious to him, the same as you are precious to me. Whenever he returns home, I barely get a hug from him before he's in the saddle and riding across town to see you."

"I'm sure you overexaggerate." Although her heart skipped a beat at Adrestia's remark.

"Ladies." The waiter arrived and set a tray on the table between them, one which held a platter covered in a silver dome—the chef's infamous custard pastries underneath. The uniformed man poured tea into two fine china cups then bowed and whisked away.

"Allow me to finish serving." Adrestia added a splash of milk to each of their cups along with two teaspoons of sugar, then nudged her cup toward her. "Now that you know what I've been up to, what about you?"

"I haven't been visiting faraway realms as you have, I'm afraid, but I have recently traveled to Hillhurst Hall near the Scottish Borders. Winterly recently spoke vows with Lady Rosamonde Raven, the Earl of Hillhurst's daughter. They're currently enjoying an extended honeymoon at Winterly Manor in the country."

"How wonderful. Your mama must be thrilled for Winterly." Adrestia clapped, the silver star-charms on her bangle tinkling at her wrist. "Speaking of your mama. How is she?"

"With all the weddings recently in our family, she's now hoping to secure a husband for me." She rearranged her emerald skirts to cover her crossed ankles, then sipped her tea. "Mama will be eager to see you now that you're home again though. Come and visit us tomorrow, then we can both hear all about your time away."

"I certainly shall. Let's take a look at these pastries." Adrestia lifted the dome from the tray and they both released a pleasurable sigh at the sweet decadence plated before them.

"Oh my, I'm drooling already." She snuck one of the plates and with her fork and spoon in hand, scooped a bite of the custard delicacy and smacked her lips together. Mmm, the custard and cream was so smooth, the raspberries sweet and syrupy, and the pastry holding it all together, beautifully light and flaky.

"This is pure heaven." Adrestia ate a mouthful, blew a kiss toward the kitchens. "*Delizioso.* I shall personally thank the chef later."

"I wish I could steal your chef away from you." Her next forkful wobbled precariously before she clamped her lips around it.

"Ha, I'd like to see you try." Adrestia giggled as she made a slashing motion with her fork, just like a warrior would with a sword. "Anteros and I would slay you before you reached the door with your stolen goods."

"Do excuse me ladies. I hope I'm not interrupting your conversation." Lord Herbarth stepped up to them, his gold silk waistcoat fastened over a ruffled white shirt, his cravat knotted at his neck and his gaze on her. "Lady Olivia, Miss Adrestia Bourbon, it is a pleasure to see you both."

"Lord Herbarth." She offered him a smile, as did Adrestia. "What a surprise to see you here."

"Word is that you visit a young lad named Wills each week at around this time, right here in these public dining rooms." He twirled the ends of his long moustache, looking gleefully proud that he'd procured that information. "I wished to ask if you'd like to join me for an evening at one of the playhouses."

"Oh, that is so kind of you."

"Does Friday evening suit?" A hopeful arch of his brow.

"My lord, I, ah—"

"Lady Olivia and I are attending a soiree at Bardington Manor on Friday," Adrestia cut in without batting an eyelash. "You haven't forgotten, have you, *Sorella*?" Her friend squeezed her hand. "We were going to attend together."

"No, I haven't forgotten at all." She offered Herbarth her most apologetic smile, ever so grateful of Adrestia's swift save. It wasn't that she didn't like Herbarth, because she sincerely did, but only as a friend. Unfortunately, tongues currently wagged about them and since she didn't wish to get caught any further in the crossfire, she'd been trying to maintain a little more distance from him. Three proposals of marriage he'd offered her thus far, and she sincerely hoped there wouldn't be a fourth. "Perhaps we might see you there, my lord?"

"You certainly shall." A wide smile as he caught her hand in farewell and pressed a kiss to her knuckles.

Chapter 3

Training his telescope on the horizon, Anteros grunted. Directly ahead a ship crested the waves with the House of Bourbon's colors flying from its mizzenmast. He handed his brass tube to Giovani and resumed his position at the wheel. "It is my father, and he is approaching at full speed."

"It's as Shira said." Giovani held the scope to his eye. "I'd been holding onto the hope she might've be wrong."

"At least I have been forewarned of this moment."

"Captain, ship on our bowsprit." A call from one of his crew on the foredeck. "What's your command?"

"Trim the sails. Draw in alongside the vessel," he ordered then handed the wheel over to Giovani before bounding downstairs to the foredeck. Men clambered up the rigging as he strode to the bow. With his white tunic open at his neck and a black silk sash knotted at his waist, he gripped the hilt of his belted saber, lifted one booted foot and rested it on a crate as Father's warship slowed and came in alongside him.

Father eyed him from the railing, his gold embroidered black jacket buttoned and neck cloth visible underneath the raised collar, his saber at his hip. His crew and Father's crew melted away and once they had, Father cocked a brow. "Son."

"Father. I hear you wish to speak to me."

"Shira?" Father asked.

"*Si.*" He waited, saying no more, just the squawk of a circling seagull riding the warm air currents above breaking the silence.

"I wish to converse with you in private. May I board?"

"As you wish." He motioned for Giovani to set the plank in place and Father bounded up and crossed the wooden beam. A thump onto his deck, then he led Father to his quarters. Once inside his private domain, he closed the door and gestured for his parent to sit in the chair angled toward his desk. His sire took his seat, while he strode to the side table and poured brandy from a decanter into two glasses. He handed one glass to Father, took his own desk chair and moved charts and maps out of the way before setting his glass down. Kicking his booted feet up onto one corner of his desk, he leaned back in his chair. "How is Mother?"

"She is in Vienna visiting her sisters. She will return to Sicily soon. We are holding a ball for Maria Cristina at the Royal Palace in Palermo. Five weeks' time. Maria Cristina hopes you'll be there, Adrestia too." Father swirled the amber liquor in his fine crystal glass and drank. "Obviously though, I'm not here to chat about balls and such."

"I didn't imagine so." Hands resting over his middle,

he rocked in his chair, boot heels scraping the polished surface of his desk.

Father leaned forward, his elbows braced on his knees, silver streaks flaring at both sides of his dark-haired head. "It's time for you to do your duty, Anteros."

"I have never ceased doing my duty. Have you not noticed how many French warships I've dispatched from these waters for you recently?" Yes, he dispatched them for the English and the Portuguese people too, but his main drive was to dispatch them for Sicily. His homeland had to remain under Bourbon rule. Father certainly couldn't lose Sicily the way he'd recently lost the throne of Naples to Napoleon.

"I'm not speaking of that duty, which you do exceedingly well by the way," Father stated with a firm nod. "I'm speaking of continuing the Bourbon dynasty. It's time for you to take a wife."

"Father, please. I will never take a wife and expose her to the dangers that surround me."

"I'm aware you've no desire to enter into matrimony, but you, like your mother and I, have responsibilities. It's time for you to provide me with grandsons."

"Francesco has already wed and sired an heir for you. He is your eldest. Only his sons matter."

"You are wrong, very wrong. Only seven of my eighteen children have survived to adulthood, and as I've seen time and time again, death can come for an heir and there is naught that can be done about it, other than to have sired more sons. That's what I've done, and that is what you must now do too. Who will inherit Paradiso Island otherwise?" His father rose and strode to his side table and poured more brandy, swirled and gulped the liquor down. "Your mother and I have already secured a wife for you."

"Pardon?" A jerk, his feet falling to the floor.

"You heard me."

He gritted his teeth. Why hadn't Shira warned him that his father would demand he marry? "Ask Leopoldo to marry her," he muttered.

"I'm asking you, Anteros, not Leopoldo." Father's nostrils flared. "I know you wish to rid Naples of Napoleon's hold on it, the same as your mother and I do. You actively aid me by sinking French warships and you fight right alongside the English, ensuring our ties with the English king remain strong. You have our country's best interests at heart and have for years, while Leopoldo still has so much to learn. He isn't yet ready to wed, while you are."

"I fight not only for our country, but for the freedom of everyone currently suffering under Napoleon's reign of terror. I would also like to point out that Napoleon detests me and wishes to be rid of me. Even should I agree to marry the lady you've secured for me, my life is filled with danger and it's doubtful I'll ever live long enough to bed her." One foot tapping, his impatience rising. "I'm surprised I'm still above the soil and not yet buried beneath it."

"Napoleon cannot send you to your death without severe repercussions from me, which he is damned aware of. That self-righteous Corsican has stretched his mighty arm far too wide, first sending Joseph Bonaparte to rule as King of Naples, then his brother-in-law, Joachim Murat. Neither Napoleon or any of his family will ever be able to take down the House of Bourbon, which is why I need you to marry. It is your duty to bear an heir and a spare. A dozen spares would be preferable."

"I am a lost prince, Father."

"My crew and yours know exactly who you are."

"My crew is loyal."

"So is mine, but you must understand me, Anteros. Your mother and I lost child after child following our marriage and when that happens, a man will do anything to ensure his remaining children don't lose their lives. You were raised on the island of Paradiso with your grandfather to ensure your safety. The same with Adrestia."

"I understand and have never disputed your decision to have us raised there. In fact, I am rather grateful for it." Slugging a mouthful, he eyed his sire. "Napoleon will be defeated. It is just a matter of time."

"Son, you have done your best in hiding your true identity to those outside of our family. You've operated within the shadows of the underworld as needed, as well as cared for Adrestia when I asked it of you. You've built your trade and fleet of ships, which now rival my own, but it's time for you to accept your birthright. I intend on claiming you as my son soon. Mark my words." Father leaned his fisted knuckles on his desk and loomed over him. "In the meantime, your mother and I have taken great pains to make politically advantageous marriages for all of our children as they've came of age. I wish for you to wed one of the Emperor of Austria's daughters, the Archduchess Clementina. Francis of Austria has agreed to the match."

"Clementina?" Shocked, he spluttered. "The emperor

had several lovely daughters, all of them archduchesses, but Clementina is one of his youngest. I visited Francis a year ago at Mother's request and I spoke to Clementina. She is still a child, a girl of twelve or thirteen."

"She's sixteen and recently had her first courses. She is now of age to marry."

"I'm not marrying a child." He'd never buckle on that issue.

"If I must order you to marry her, then I—"

"No."

"Do not defy me on this. You will agree." Blue eyes darkening to sharp points.

"My answer is still no." He shoved to his feet and met Father eye to eye. "How about I offer you a compromise?" If he didn't, Father would continue to press his point and he'd never be rid of him. A plan began to bloom in his mind. Shira had said to follow his instincts. Those consisted of undertaking an elaborate ruse, of speaking false marriage vows with a willing accomplice. Luckily, he had an angel who owed him a favor. "Since you insist I wed, then allow me to choose my own bride."

"Explain." A roll of Father's shoulders, suspicion still in his eyes.

"I don't actually want to admit this, but I am currently intrigued by an English lady who I would have no issue bedding." The truth so far.

"Hmm." A tick of the muscle in Father's jaw. "English you say? Do you mean from the Royal House of Hanover?"

"No, she isn't royalty, but she is from a strong and loyal line."

"Give me her name."

"Lady Olivia Trentbury. She is the Earl of Winterly's sister." A little more of Father's suspicion seemed to lift, so he continued, "She is the only woman I would ever consider entering into matrimony with."

"You will wed her, bed her, and get her with child?"

"I would if there was no other choice."

"I see." Father stroked his jaw, breathed deep, and nodded. "I will accept the English lady as your bride, although if you don't do as you've proclaimed, then I will bring you to heel by whatever means I must. Do not fail me. Am I understood?"

"There is no need to use threats against me, Father."

"That wasn't a threat, Son. It was a promise." Father strode to the door, opened it and glanced at him over his shoulder. "I will leave one of my men on board your ship. Signore Piero Bruno. Bruno will report back to me once he's witnessed your vows being spoken, which of course must take place on Paradiso since those are the stipulations handed down by your grandfather before his death."

"I'm aware I can't marry anywhere else, other than where I was born and raised."

"Good." Father left, closing the door behind him.

He could handle one spy, for that's exactly what Bruno would be, an unwanted presence tailing him day and night until he'd done the deed and spoken marriage vows with Olivia. Well, those vows would happen, but they wouldn't be legal or binding. He'd ensure it. It was time to speak to his angel and call in a debt.

Hopefully, she wouldn't turn him down, not in his greatest time of need.

Chapter 4

Two weeks later in her bedchamber before the cozy warmth of her fire, Olivia readied for the masquerade ball being held that evening at Brightson House, Mama chaperoning both her and Adrestia since Anteros hadn't yet returned from sea as expected.

She swirled her favorite orange blossom bath oil into the water and after disrobing, stepped into the wooden tub and settled down. She dunked her head under the water, came up and worked a bar of soap into a mass of citrusy bubbles. With the suds in hand, she scrubbed her hair, dunked under again and rinsed.

Resting her wet head on the rim, she relaxed back as the fire crackled, the flames glowing a vibrant orange-red. As she raised her toes above the surface, water sluiced off her feet, the drops running in rivulets down her calves before splashing back into the tub.

A whoosh of her hand over the surface and the water rippled. The undulating wave swept to the side of the tub and cascaded back.

She'd always enjoyed playing in the water, ever since her earliest years. As a child, she'd stamp through puddles, swim in the shallows at the seaside, and lift her face to the skies when it rained. Her first memory of being out on the water flickered to life. Five years of age, she'd been at the time, sitting in a rowboat with Papa, just the two of them out enjoying a warm spring day a hundred feet from the lake shore. Mama had been lazing on the sandy verge with a book since she suffered from terrible seasickness and wouldn't even step one foot onto a ship, let alone a wobbly rowboat.

That lake very near their country estate had been Papa's favorite spot to fish in, private and serene. That day Papa had hooked a wriggly worm on the end of her line as bait, and she'd tossed the line over the side then waited with giddy anticipation for a bite. When a fish had caught and tugged, she'd barely been able to sit still, which had made Papa chuckle at her excitement. Papa had helped her reel her first fish in that day, and later that evening they'd eaten it for—

"May I come in, my lady?" A knock rattled her door, made her splash upright in her tub.

"Yes, please do." Best she get out and cease dawdling. She had a masked ball to attend, one she'd been looking forward to for several weeks. She rose and got swamped in the drying cloth Lucy wrapped around her. A quick rub dry and she eased into her dressing robe, tied the sash and sat before her dressing table.

Lucy collected her brush and standing at her back, gently brushed her hair until her locks dried from the warmth of the fire into a shiny fall of golden-blond. "Madam Gonnier has outdone herself with your costume for the ball, my lady. It is absolutely divine."

"Would you lay it out on the bed for me?"

"Of course." Her maid crossed to her wardrobe, collected her gown and draped it over the end of her four-poster bed, the lacy white fabric stark against her cherry-colored bedcovers. "The madam has even created angel wings for you to attach to the ensemble. She is a master at what she does." Lucy carefully collected the silk undergarment and the wings from atop a corner trunk and placed them on the bed too. "The modiste explained to me exactly how I was to attach the wings."

"Then aid me dressing. I'm eager to see the costume all put together." She shrugged out of her dressing gown and lifted her arms. Lucy slid the undergarment over her head and the skin-colored silk of the lining rippled down her body with the softest caress before brushing the white woolen rug gracing her polished floorboards. Next came the fine white lace overlay of the gown and once her maid had fastened the line of pearl buttons running down her spine, she stepped in front of her tall-standing cheval mirror and did a twirl. The lace swept into a short train at the back with dainty white flowers embroidered along the scalloped edge, while crystals sewn into the lace glittered like stars in the night sky. At first glance it appeared as if she wore naught underneath the fine lace, what with the lining matching her skin tone to perfection.

"It is stunning, very angelic." Lucy fixed the feathery white angel wings in place, the filaments glittering along the upper curves and lower fall of the wings where more crystals had been added. A gasp as her maid covered her mouth. "Oh, my lady, you look magnificent."

"Thank you for saying so." She turned this way and that to get a better look at the wings in the mirror.

"You're almost ready. Gloves and slippers next, then your hair." Lucy drew the lacy white gloves on her fingers, crouched and held the matching white slippers out for her to slide her feet into, then she patted the chair before her dressing table. "Come and sit. How would you like your hair arranged for the night?"

"In theme, as you would imagine an angel's hair to appear."

"I picked some sprigs of small white flowers earlier. I'll fetch them now and fashion them into a crown atop your head. They'll look like an angelic halo." Her maid dashed out the door, then returned a few minutes later with the flowers in hand.

Lucy swept her golden locks into a fanciful arrangement with side braids curling upward around a top knot. She added the dainty white flowers in a circular crown then finished off her creation with a few loose curls dangling free down her nape. The arrangement was soft and sultry and absolutely perfect.

"You've outdone yourself, Lucy." She opened the lid of her wooden jewelry box which Papa had made for her as a child and selected her favorite gold earrings to complement her locket. She stroked the engraving of the cobra at her neck, Anteros's diamond hidden safely away inside.

"I'll aid you with your mask." Lucy held the white feather and silk mask with great care as she fitted it over her eyes and secured it in place at the back with silk ties.

Another knock and Mama breezed in wearing a woodland fairy inspired gown with pleated forest-green skirts and matching bodice, her mask a glittery tinge of the same color with a quiver of feathers spanning in a spritely arch across the sweeping rise of her top knot. Woodland-colored fairy wings bobbed from Mama's back, and as she waved a wand, Mama appeared every inch a fairy godmother. "You look wonderful, Mama."

"And you look divine, my child, just like an angel sent from the heavens. I wish your dear papa could see how you've blossomed into such a beautiful young lady. He would be immensely proud of you." A tear shimmered in Mama's eyes.

"Thank you for saying so. I love you." She kissed Mama's warm cheeks, first her left, then her right. "I hope I marry a man as loving and as honorable as Papa was." She linked arms with Mama and crossed to the door which Lucy held open for them.

"Do you consider Lord Herbarth a contender for your hand?" Mama asked as she led the way down the hallway. "I realize he's proposed three times and that you've turned him down three times too, but you continue to dance with him at every ball we attend."

"He's polite and kind and devastated over the loss of his mother. Since I know what it's like to lose a parent, I've tried to be a friend, but it is difficult learning what distance to keep so that the brunt of any gossip remains at bay." She gently stroked her locket, which caught Mama's astute gaze.

"It's impossible to miss that you still hold onto

Captain Bourbon's diamond." Mama's gaze softened. "The captain is an honorable man and neither Winterly or I will ever forget how he has come to the aid of our family whenever needed. He is heroic, and we will always hold him in great esteem." Mama grasped the handrail as they walked downstairs, then at the base of the stairs Mama glanced at her under her lashes. "Did I mention Captain Bourbon has returned?"

"No." Halting, she shook her head. "Surely he hasn't." She'd gone riding with Adrestia just yesterday and her friend would have told her if Anteros had sailed into port. Not only that, but Anteros would have paid a call to her and Mama upon his return, unless of course he'd only arrived today. "When did he make berth?"

"This afternoon, only a few short hours ago. He has arrived here with Adrestia this eve. They're both in our drawing room, the captain having offered to take us in his carriage tonight."

"You should have said sooner." Surprised and excited, she could barely restrain her emotions as she hurried down the passageway. She skidded into the drawing room in a most unladylike fashion, then grateful her mask currently hid her expression, she openly ogled Anteros where he stood next to the fireplace, a brandy glass in hand and his gaze on the flames. He was dressed head to toe in domino with a hood covering his dark head and wide sleeves enveloping his arms. Gold brocade ran down the front buttoning of his robe, adding a touch of finesse to his costume, while a black silk mask covered the top half of his face.

"Captain Bourbon," she murmured a little roughly, one

hand clutched to her chest. "Welcome home."

He slowly turned, his blue eyes going wide through his eye-slits, the brandy sloshing the rim of his glass as he openly stared at her. Gulping for a breath, he squeezed his eyes tightly shut and didn't move, not an inch, his chest rising and falling sharply, his breath coming harder.

"Anteros? Are you all right?" His sister rose from the blue brocade settee where she sat, her midnight-black hair lying sleek and straight with an Egyptian crown upon her head and a masterfully fitted golden gown clinging to her body. A glittering Cleopatra mask covered Adrestia's cheeks and nose, her heavily lashed eyes peeking out through her eye-slits. Gripping her brother's arm, she nudged him. "Is something wrong, *Fratello*?"

"Not at all." A squeaky answer, then he rattled off a long length of Italian before he opened his eyes once more, his gaze going straight to Mama. "Lady Winterly, you look divine, as does your daughter."

"I'm so glad you arrived back in England in time to attend the Brightson House ball with us this eve, and of course for your gracious offer to drive us there," Mama gushed as she joined Bourbon and Adrestia at the hearth. Grasping Adrestia's hands, Mama beamed. "My dear, you make a stunning Cleopatra, a woman who was born to rule, a true queen in every sense. Let me see the entire creation."

"Of course." Adrestia lifted her arms and twirled about, the sheer golden fabric flowing like silken ivory wings from her shoulders to her wrists, while a golden-tasseled belt knotted at her waist shimmered in the firelight.

"Oh, the Egyptians are most fortunate to have you seated upon their throne this night, Adrestia. Come, I am eagerly awaiting this eve's soiree. Let us be away." Mama steered Adrestia from the room, the two of them disappearing down the passageway, their chatter echoing back.

"You look very handsome in your costume, sir." With her hands clasped in front, she tried not to twist her fingers together as she met Anteros's gaze.

"I apologize for not greeting you properly, but you quite stunned me with how radiant you look. *Bellissimo. Prezioso. Angelico.*" Huskily spoken words. "Are you well?"

"I am in good health, yes. What of you?"

"It has been a difficult few weeks while I've been at sea." He straightened his shoulders, his regal bearing proud and strong and tall.

"Then it is just as well you're now home again." She moved toward him, the train of her gown rustling across the deep blue carpet of the drawing room, her angel wings fluttering. When he remained silent, she asked, "How long will you be enjoying a sojourn in London for?"

"I'm afraid not long. I must set sail again soon." He caught her hand, lifted it to his lips and pressed a sweet kiss against her knuckles. "But not until after you and I have spoken in private. I have a great deal I need to discuss with you."

"That sounds intriguing." She caught the glimmer of his medallion within the front folds of his black robe, lifted it free and squeezed her fingers around it. A gentle tug as she drew him closer, and when he swallowed hard, she smiled. "Do I scare you, Captain?"

"You terrify me."

"Perfect, that has always been my aim, to terrify *the cobra*. You also need more time on land, to rest and recuperate and enjoy being with friends and family. Come riding with me tomorrow morning. Adrestia and I have already arranged to meet here at ten for an excursion to Hyde Park. Surely your stallion requires a run now his master is home?"

"See, that is exactly why you terrify me. With absolute ease you manage to bend me to your will. Of course I'll come." He leaned in closer, his warm breath caressing her cheeks either side of her mask and fluttering the bobbing curls at her neck. "I thought about you all the time while I was away. Do you have any suitors already holding dances for tonight's ball?"

"One or two." She'd made promises, as she always did. "Lord Fellows and Lord Herbarth."

"Herbarth again?" He released a low growl under his breath. "That man simply won't stay away from you. Does he continue to propose marriage as well?"

"Only the three proposals so far, but since he's certain I'll capitulate one day, there will likely be more."

"*Bastardo*." He slammed one fisted hand into the other. "I will warn him tonight to remain clear of you once and for all. I will not tolerate—"

"No, that will only cause a great deal of gossip if you do, not that I don't appreciate your offer." Her captain sometimes forgot when he wasn't at sea that he couldn't simply dispatch his enemy by wielding his blade.

"Olivia, dear!" Mama's call reached her from the foyer.

"Coming," she called back. "We shouldn't keep them

waiting."

"No, we shouldn't." He extended his arm. "I brought my carriage. May I escort you to it?"

"You certainly may." She'd allow him to escort her anywhere.

If only he would but ask...

Chapter 5

Anteros walked down the driveway with his angel at his side and motioned for her to step into his awaiting coach. With his sister and Lady Winterly already seated on the rear padded seat together, he eased onto the front seat of plush golden velvet padding and with a tap to the roof, called out to his driver, "To Brightson House."

The slap of the reins echoed, and they lurched forward. The horses soon settled into a smooth gait as they journeyed the streets toward the hive of stately homes near St James's Park. Out the carriage window the skies darkened further, the moon rising behind a layer of cloud.

"Are the night skies you sail at sea the same in beauty as the ones upon land?" Olivia asked in his ear, her hand on the squabs between them, her fingers so close to brushing against his fingers.

"The sunsets in the Mediterranean are the most radiant I've ever beheld, particularly when the array of colors long the horizon ripple across the surface of the sea as well." He kept his gaze out his window for fear of looking into her eyes again. If he did, he'd likely sink into the sweet oblivion of them, just as he'd done when she'd arrived in the drawing room.

He'd tried to prepare himself on the ride to her home for when he first saw her again, but when she'd swept around the corner, he'd gotten completely lost in the returned sight of her. She'd glided toward him with her heavenly body clothed in what had appeared as naught more than white lace and nothing underneath. A trick of the eye. It wasn't until he'd caught the glimmer of her skin-colored lining that he'd finally been able to breathe again. Hell, she'd dressed as an angel—incredibly fitting.

Right now, her glittery wings were pressed to the padded backrest, one of them currently trapped behind his own back. Somehow that brought a sense of comfort to him, that she couldn't move any farther away from him unless he moved first.

Carefully, from the corner of one eye-slit, he chanced a look at her. The full swell of her breasts rose higher with each breath she drew in, the golden locket engraved with his insignia nestled so sweetly between both creamy mounds. No woman had ever attempted to align herself so physically with him the way she'd done. Her eldest brother had complained about it once. Winterly had taken him aside after learning his sister held his diamond inside her locket. He'd been quizzed about his relationship with Olivia, Winterly stating no lady should accept jewelry from any man other than her husband. He'd stated quite clearly in return that he had no intention of ever requesting the diamond be returned, not when it adorned the neck of such an exquisite angel.

"Oh, look at that," Olivia pointed as they rounded a corner, her hand brushing his chest as she reached across toward the window. A long line of carriages graced cither side of the street. "Well, there will certainly be a large crowd tonight."

"Brightson House is magnificent and will do justice to such a crowd." Adrestia scanned the palatial building up ahead, their coach moving slowly forward in short spurts as they awaited their turn to draw up to the entrance. "One cannot attend such events as these when sailing the seas." His sister smiled sweetly at him. "I'm glad you returned in time for the masquerade, *Fratello.*"

"As am I, *Sorella.*" Particularly after seeing Olivia in her costume. He needed to keep the gentlemen who would be inundating her with requests to dance, as far away from her as possible. Breathing deep, he pushed the window open a notch. The snorting of the horses and the rattle of the wheels traveled to him. Brightson House stood a magnificent three stories high, its front windows ablaze with candlelight and liveried footmen attending to guests as they stepped clear of their carriages.

When they came to a complete halt, he opened the door and stepped down before offering each of the ladies a hand onto the cobbled pathway. The excited chatter of the guests ahead swept over them as they walked together and entered the front doors.

The grand foyer stood two floors high with radiant chandeliers and a sweeping staircase either side. A mosaic of stained-glass windows shimmered with vivid reds, ellows and blues, the white tiled floor crammed with people. Carefully, he led the ladies toward the grand arch leading into the ballroom where a veritable crush circulated around the edge of the dancefloor. Olivia and his sister accepted dance cards from a uniformed servant, then the four of them entered the main room and eased around the fringes as couples took their places for the first dance of the night.

"Oh, I see Lady Foxeworth at the refreshment table." Lady Winterly squeezed Olivia's hand. "I must speak with her before I lose her in this crowd."

"Go right ahead, Mama. You've been meaning to speak to her all week."

"Thank you, my dear. I knew you'd understand." Lady Winterly bustled away, heading directly toward an older woman wearing a bold peacock-colored costume with a spray of peacock feathers adorning her mask.

His sister cooled herself with her delicate white-feathered fan before accepting a fluted glass of champagne from a passing waiter, although Olivia declined as her dance card fluttered to the floor. She scooped it up and valiantly tried to tie the laces more securely to her wrist.

"Allow me." He slipped the card from her gloved fingers and looked into her stunning golden eyes as he tied the laces into a bow. With so many people surrounding them, it was easy enough to lean in closer, his next words only for her. "You must reserve every dance for me."

"I couldn't possibly do that." Her lush lips lifted into a brilliant smile, the corners of her mouth disappearing up behind her pretty mask.

"I will wield my blade against any gentleman who dares to sign your card otherwise." He shoved one side of his robe clear of his belted saber and rested his palm on the gilded hilt. He never went anywhere without being incredibly well armed. Daggers were sheathed at his wrist and his ankle, a pistol tucked away in his pocket.

"I believe you would too." She pressed a hand against his chest, nudged him gently back.

Which he didn't care for, not one bit. He wanted to be closer to her, not farther away.

"*Fratello.*" Adrestia touched his arm, pulled his attention to her, the music and chatter from the crowd drifting over them. "Bruno is here tonight." She gave him a subtle cue with an arch of one brow toward the far shadowed corner.

Beyond the dancing couples twirling under the shimmering candlelight, his father's man indeed stood in the far shadows wearing a black satin cloak over black evening attire, the jagged scar which slashed one side of his face clearly evident above and below his eye mask.

As soon as he and Giovani had arrived home, he'd taken his sister and right-hand man aside and spoken to them both at length about his conversation with Father. Neither had been surprised about Father's demand, or that Bruno had been placed on board his ship to tail him. They had though been surprised when he'd outlined his plan about speaking false marriage vows with Olivia, about making Father believe he had wed her even though he hadn't. He needed time, and this coming ruse he intended on instigating would provide that.

"I want you to waylay Bruno for me." He cocked a brow at Adrestia. "I'll whisk Olivia away so I can speak to her in private about my plan."

"You should consider proposing to her in truth, not offering her a false engagement which she can't speak about to another. Think about it."

"I'm not changing my mind on the matrimony front." He'd never take a wife, not when he'd only be exposing said wife to the dangers that surrounded him.

"As you wish." A long sigh as Adrestia reached up on her toes and kissed his cheek. "Where is Giovani?"

"Securing the library for me."

"Very good. I'll go and keep Bruno busy." A little deflated, his sister disappeared into the crush as she weaved her way around the fringe of the ballroom toward their spy. He understood her subdued look, particularly when she considered Olivia more than a friend. Olivia was like a sister to Adrestia, the two of them as thick as thieves whenever here in town together.

"Come with me, *mio angelo*." He caught Olivia's gloved hand, hooked it through his bent arm and steered her through the closest side door.

"Where are we going?" She gasped as she glanced back at the ballroom. "The dancefloor is back there."

"We're going to the library to resume our conversation from earlier." He passed the open door to the games room where beyond the door guests sat around tables playing cards, a fire blazing and spreading its warmth through the room and into the passageway.

"Which conversation was that?"

"The one I mentioned in your drawing room. I have a great deal I need to discuss with you, in private of course." Along a labyrinth of candlelit passageways, he walked until he reached the stairwell leading upstairs to the library on the second floor. He ascended the stairs with Olivia on his arm, rounded a corner and gestured to the closed library door. "Giovani will ensure we aren't interrupted."

"Giovani isn't here." She frowned, darting a look in both directions of the darkened hallway. "Giovani?" she called out quietly.

"My lady, how are you this evening?" Dressed in domino, Giovani eased out from a shadowed doorway.

"I'm well." She fluttered a hand over her heart. "You turn up in all sorts of strange places."

"My apologies." He swept forward and opened the library door. "The fire is lit, the room warm and secure, and please be assured I'll keep any unwanted guests from disturbing you."

"Thank you, Giovani." Anteros urged Olivia into the library and closed the door before his angel had the chance to change her mind.

It was time to unveil his plan.

Chapter 6

Olivia lifted her hands to the warmth of the logs crackling in the library's fireplace, rather surprised at the sudden turn of events. She had no idea what Anteros wanted to speak to her about, particularly which required him stealing her away from the ballroom where their disappearance might be noticed by others.

"If you remove your gloves, you'll feel the warmth of the fire better." Anteros pushed his hood back, unbuttoned his robe and shrugged out of it before laying it over the armrest of the nearest cream brocade padded armchair. Next, he removed his mask, dropped it on top and ambled over to a side table holding fluted glasses and a bottle of wine. He held the chilled bottle toward her for her inspection. "Do you care for a glass?"

"Yes, please. I'm parched." She plucked her gloves free, lifted her mask from her face and set her belongings on the armchair, just as he'd done. "I don't believe I've seen that marker on a wine bottle before." The letters PV were enclosed within a snakelike wreath. "Where has it come from?"

"Paradiso Vineyards, which is located on an island just off the coastline of Sicily." He removed the cork and poured a glass. "I always bring an entire case back after visiting the island. Giovani had the bottle chilled and placed here for us tonight." He set the bottle down and handed her the stemmed flute he'd filled. "Try it. Tell me what you think."

"I'm not a wine connoisseur, not by any means." She sipped delicately from the rim, the wine a fruity and exotically smooth blend. A lick of her lips, which drew his gaze to her mouth, his sapphire eyes darkening in the firelit room. "Mmm, but this is certainly delicious. One doesn't need to be an authority on wines to recognize that."

"It is certainly delicious watching you drink it." He touched a thumb to her lower lip, drew the wetness of the wine away and outrageously, stuck his thumb in his mouth and sucked the drop.

"You are an outrageous flirt." She gulped another mouthful, a whole lot breathless.

"I'm simply stating a fact." He lifted her free hand and pressed it against his cheek, then he tipped his nose into her palm and breathed deep, as if taking in her scent. "You smell edible, of exotic citrus fruits."

"I added scented orange blossom oil to my bathwater tonight."

"How intriguing." He removed her glass from her fingertips, sipped from the rim right where she'd sipped, then set the glass on the table before returning his gaze to her. "You are far too trusting, allowing yourself to be left alone in a room with me."

"You would never hurt me." Which they'd established a very long time ago. She touched the ends of his gloriously silky black hair sweeping across his shoulders, his snowy white cravat foaming at his neck and his medallion glinting within the ruffles. Releasing a soft sigh, she did what she'd never done with him before and leaned in, rested her cheek against his chest and allowed his warmth to envelop her. Goodness, but such an incredible sense of rightness hummed through her.

He didn't move, not a single inch, although his heartbeat pounded under her ear and his next words floated deliciously across the top of her head, "*Non capisco i sentimenti che ho per te, ma sono infinitamente profondi.*"

"That will require a translation." A nuzzle against his chest.

He remained silent, neither of them moving, the air between them fairly crackling.

"Tell me what you just said, Anteros."

Another long minute passed, as if he didn't wish to answer her, then he cleared his throat. "I said, I don't understand the feelings I have for you, but they are endlessly deep."

"Would they be feelings of friendship...or something more?" She lifted her head, searched his gaze. "Be honest with me."

"Honesty isn't always helpful." He kissed her forehead, asked, "Will you dance with me?"

"I can't hear the music from here."

"One doesn't always need to hear music in order to dance. Within the desert lands of Algiers, the women first learn to sway their hips to the beat of their own hearts." He captured one of her hands, curled it over his shoulder then holding her other hand, drew her into a soft sway, his hips so closely aligned against her hips. "We shall dance like this, *si?*"

"Yes." She looked deep into his eyes. "How does a lady say in Italian, 'Thank you for the dance?'"

"*Grazie per il ballo.*"

"*Grazie per il ballo.*" She repeated his words with a smile.

"You speak perfect Italian."

"I wish I did." A giggle escaped her. "Will you teach me more?"

"I could." Leaning into her ear, he whispered, "*Sarai mia?*"

"*Sarai mia?*" she whispered in return, barely able to get those two words out due to the carnal way he'd spoken them. "What does that mean?"

"Will you be mine?" Such a devilishly wide smile.

"Anteros." She growled his name. "You are meant to be teaching me words I can say to other people. What if I opened that door and whispered those words to Giovani thinking it was completely acceptable?"

"I would be forced to slice his ears off. It isn't acceptable for him to hear such words coming from your sweet lips." He tipped her back off her feet, one arm firm around her back, his gaze locked with hers.

"You are a scoundrel." Heat flared through her in all sorts of places. Her cheeks, her chest, her middle, even between her legs. "This is not a dance I've ever partaken of. It is scandalous."

"Then you need to visit Algiers."

"I can't, not unless you offer to take me there." She gave him a challenging look.

"Now who is being the scandalous one, inviting me to steal you away so you can explore the world with me?"

"I doubt there would be any stealing involved. I'd gladly travel the world with you." Never had she spoken so outrageously, but it was the truth, and it also felt incredibly freeing to state it. "I've yet to meet any of your family, other than Adrestia of course. I know you have brothers and sisters." Both he and Adrestia had mentioned siblings here and there over the past year a half. "When two people are friends such as you and I are, it is normal for them to wish to get to know each other better, to speak of their families, their common interests, likes and dislikes. What they might desire. What they hope for their future."

"My one and only desire for the future is for this blasted war to end, for Napoleon to be brought to trial for his misdeeds, then punished accordingly." He righted her back on her feet and resumed swaying, her body flush against his.

"Well, we all hope for that." If only he would open up further, to allow her more of a glimpse into who he truly was. "The Cobra is a formidable vessel. How did you come to acquire her and the remainder of your fleet? You've never told me that story."

"There is no story. I acquired my fleet through the shedding of blood, sweat, and tears. Mine, and my men's."

Still not a true answer, so she pushed harder. "Did you commission The Cobra's build? Win it in a game of cards? Sequester it from another at sea?"

"You believe I am a buccaneer who sails the seas thieving whatever I may?"

"Do you consider yourself a buccaneer, Captain Bourbon?" He simply grinned at her, the cad, an infuriating grin she couldn't help but smile at too. "You are impossible. I want to get to know you, not the rake and rascal you often purport yourself to be."

"There is no purporting. I am a rake and a rascal."

"Then speak of the discussion you wished to have with me, the one which requires complete privacy between us here in the library."

"*Sì*, we must speak of that important issue immediately." He released her, slowly lowered to one knee, one of her hands still held in his firm grip.

"What are you doing?" Shocked, she could barely lug in a breath. A man never went down on bended knee unless he had the desire to offer a proposal of marriage. "Please, I—"

"It's only right I ask this question at your feet." He cleared his throat. "Lady Olivia Trentbury, I'd like to request your hand in marriage."

"I—I—" She swayed, black dots dancing everywhere.

Chapter 7

"Olivia?" Anteros remained on one knee as the color drained from Olivia's face and she went completely ashen.

"D-did—" She opened her mouth, closed it again, then blinked repeatedly. "Did you just ask me to marry you?"

"I did. Allow me to explain why." He surged back to his feet and taking her hand, tugged her across to the elegant wine-red settee in front of the wall of redwood library shelves holding beautiful leather-bound books. Once he'd settled her on the settee, he eased down and faced her. "I once told you that the seer, Shira Ria, informed me that you and I are destined to continually cross paths."

"Yes, I recall that day when you spoke of her. We were in the museum."

"Well, Shira has recently read my future again and she saw that I would soon have a conversation with my father, one that would result in a change, one that would ensure heartache if I adhered to my father's request. Shira advised me instead to follow my instincts on the issue, which I did."

"That still doesn't make any sense."

"My father wishes to force a politically arranged marriage on me, one to a girl of sixteen."

A shocked gasp. "Sixteen is young."

"She is the Emperor of Austria's daughter, the Archduchess Clementina, and I fully agree, sixteen is too young. Which is why I've come up with a plan to circumvent any marriage from happening. My request for your hand actually comes as a plea, one that will not end in actual marriage vows being spoken."

"Your marriage proposal to me is a ploy?" Her gaze went wide. "Oh, I'm a decoy? Correct?"

"Yes. If I wish to be rid of Father and this forced marriage, then I need your aid in being a decoy."

"My family owes you a great debt, one I've always wished to repay. I'm listening." She settled back, folded her hands in her lap, the flickering flames of the fire casting a golden light over her, the glow caressing her angelic wings and sparkling off the embedded crystals. "Please continue."

Thankfully, she was still listening. Now, to outline his plan.

"My father can be a beast at times, even if he means well, so I have reached an agreement with him, that I would take an English lady as my wife. I gave him your name and stated you were the only lady to whom I'd ever consider entering into holy matrimony with." He rose and collected the glass of wine, returned and handed it to her, his knees bumping into hers on the settee. "He's well aware I've no desire to marry at all, has even placed a spy in my midst to ensure I go through with the ceremony. Signore Piero Bruno is my father's man who currently tails me. He is downstairs as we speak, Adrestia keeping him occupied so I might have this conversation with you."

"Adrestia knows about all of this?"

"Yes, Giovani too. You see arranged marriages are the accepted form of marriage in my family line. Father himself wed my mother out of duty, and out of duty my mother accepted him as her husband."

"Many marriages are made out of duty, with girls from Society barely into their first Season before finding themselves engaged and planning their weddings. Sixteen though." She sipped her wine, handed the fluted glass back to him. "That is a terribly young age to be taking on the duty of being a wife."

"I've no desire to be a husband to one so young either, nor to take a wife at all. Not when that would only expose her to my dangerous activities out at sea." He gulped a mouthful then cradled the drink between his legs, elbows to his knees. "What I need to know is if you would consider speaking false marriage vows with me? I do have a plan."

"Please, enlighten me."

"Well, if you agree to offering me your aid, then first you would need to sail with me to the island of Paradiso."

"Where the wine came from?" She tapped the glass in his hands.

"Yes, the island used to belong to my grandfather, being unentailed land that he passed directly onto me following his death. Adrestia and I were raised there. A stipulation in Grandfather's will ensures that Paradiso is the only place where either she or I can legally marry, which comes directly from the unusual circumstances surrounding our births. Grandfather also decreed one further condition, primarily to ensure no one could dispute the legality of any marriage my sister and I entered into, either under Naples or Sicilian law. That condition is that one of my immediate family members must be present at the ceremony when the vows are spoken. That shall be Adrestia, if you agree to my plan."

"I see." A slow nod. "How do you intend to ensure the marriage isn't legitimate?"

"We'll be speaking false marriage vows." Gently, he touched the backs of his fingers to the creamy soft skin of her cheek. "I've considered your reputation while constructing my plan, and of how I shall keep it firmly intact."

"Go ahead."

"I came prepared." He placed the wine glass on the floor by his feet, removed a sealed missive from the pocket of his tailored breeches and handed it to her. "This invitation is from Maria Cristina, the Duchess of Genoa who is currently residing in Sicily at the Royal Palace of Palermo, her parents' home. It is an invitation for you to spend time at the palace and to attend the forthcoming ball in the duchess's honor."

"Surely you jest?" Shock widened her eyes, then excitement shimmered in their golden depths. "I've heard word of the ball, even from these faraway shores. How on earth did you secure such a sought-after invitation for me?"

"The duchess owed me a favor. Both you and Adrestia have invites."

"Oh my." She traced one finger over the royal seal

embedded into the red wax, slid her finger under the seal and unfolded the thick piece of parchment, the invite lavishly styled with Olivia's name prominent on the first line. Her hands trembled. "I can barely believe I'm holding onto this. Mama would never allow me to decline such a sought-after invitation, although I'll need a suitable chaperone of course. My maid. A footman too who could serve as my guard on the journey."

"You don't wish to ask your mama to sail with us as your chaperone?" He had no issue if she did. He'd find a way to explain things—the ruse—to her mama.

"No, she cannot tolerate being on water. She suffers from terrible sea sickness whenever forced to sail." She refolded the invite. "It would be best if I kept the actual truth about this whole ruse from her, otherwise Mama will only worry unnecessarily."

"Does that mean you're agreeing to my plan?"

"It does, yes. I shall indeed speak false marriage vows with you, Anteros. You've done so much for my family and I simply can't step away when you have such a great need. I do have a question though. Will you be rid of Bruno once we speak these false marriage vows on Paradiso?"

"I will, and hopefully I'll never have to come into contact with Bruno again."

"This is almost unbelievable." She jiggled about on the settee, a giddy laugh escaping her. "I shall soon see the Mediterranean and faraway lands, which shall be a dream come true. I've always wished to spread my wings and experience all the world has to offer, and now here you are offering me that exact possibility, albeit with an unusual request on the side."

"So I should consider myself engaged?" Had she truly agreed to his request?

"Yes, you may, falsely engaged of course." She rose from the settee, crossed the carpeted floor of woven reds and blues, released the ribbon on her dance card and tossed it into the crackling flames of the fire. Returning to him, her sweet orange blossom scent surrounding him, she twirled about. "I suddenly feel free."

"*Grazie.* I can't thank you enough for your agreement." He rose and caught her around her waist. He'd gotten his wish tonight. "I am the luckiest man on—"

A scuffle erupted in the hallway, loud voices and gruff growls echoing.

He whisked Olivia in behind him and slid his saber from his scabbard just as the door burst open. Bruno stormed in with Giovani hard on his heels. He pressed his blade to the spy's thick neck, Giovani's blade pressed to the man's nape.

Bruno snarled, his upper lip curled, his mask removed and his black cloak swaying about his legs. "I'm under strict orders to keep you under my watch."

"I don't require a man to watch me, not every second of every day." Anger thrummed through him. He wanted to slice Bruno's head from his shoulders. "I also wouldn't advise moving, not even an inch, not if you want to keep your head."

"Anteros?" Olivia pressed against his back, the warmth of her body calming him a little. "Who is this man who dares to interrupt us?"

"An *idiota.*" Nudging the pointed tip of his blade, he broke Bruno's skin and a thin line of blood dribbled down and soaked his black cravat. He wouldn't tolerate Bruno throwing his weight around. "You have until the count of three to leave. One."

A vein throbbed across Bruno's wide forehead, then without another word the man swung around and stormed from the room.

"*Mie scuse.*" Giovani dipped his head in apology, backed out of the room and closed the door with barely a snick.

Sheathing his blade, he faced Olivia. "My apologies too. That won't happen again. Giovani will ensure it."

"That wasn't your fault." Meeting his gaze, she stepped closer, until the tips of her slippers touched the tips of his booted feet. "Your saber was in your hand before I could even blink. I've never witnessed anyone moving that fast before."

"If a man doesn't move fast…he might die."

"Do you ever lay your weapons aside?"

"No." He'd never met a lady who wouldn't be trembling at least a little after what she'd just witnessed. Instead, she offered him a soft smile before wandering across to the square-cut windows framed by wine-red damask drapes.

With her hands pressed to the windowsill, she gazed out over the rear gardens, the night sky having cleared of the darkened clouds and now showcasing a heavenly cascade of twinkling stars within the realm of midnight blue. A light wind blew in from one partially open window, the soft breeze fluttering her golden locks and her angelic wings, the white lace overlay of her gown lit a gentle gold by the moonlight.

Needing to be closer to her, he crossed the distance separating them.

He crowded her from behind, swept her hair over one winged shoulder and stuck his nose against the soft skin of her neck. Tiny pearl buttons ran down the length of her spine and with one hand on her hip, he rubbed against her. She had such ripe curves. He nibbled on her earlobe, skimmed his hand around to her belly and caressed the smooth line of her middle.

"Anteros?" Sucking in a breath, she leaned back against him. "You make me feel things I've never felt with another man before."

"Have you ever allowed a man to get this close to you?" He ran his tongue along the soft whorls of her ear.

"No, there have always been boundaries I've never crossed." She tipped her head back against his shoulder, her eyes closing and golden eyelashes sweeping down onto her flushed cheeks.

"I haven't taken a lover in over eighteen months." He wasn't sure why he'd just admitted that, other than that it seemed important she was aware.

"Not since before we met?" She lifted one hand and curled it around his neck, the upper swells of her breasts rising as she stretched onto her toes.

"*Sì.*" He'd forged a bond with her from the beginning, and even though they'd agreed to be friends and naught more, he'd still had the devil of a time trying to allow another woman's touch. Of course, eager barmaids in taverns would wiggle their bottoms and jiggle their breasts at him, but he never took them up on their blatant offers.

"I kissed a man not long ago," she blurted.

"Who?" Anger didn't even begin to express the emotion which suddenly rose within him.

"I thought kissing would be magical, to share breath with another and for them to share theirs in return. Obviously, I kissed the wrong man." She turned in his arms and searched his gaze. "Would you show me what kissing is truly meant to be like?"

"It would be best if I didn't." He hadn't missed how she'd ignored his last question of whom she'd kissed, but perhaps it was best he didn't know since that would only mean the night wouldn't end for him without a manhunt underway.

"Please, Anteros, will you kiss me?" She licked her lips, wetting them in the most enticing way, her golden eyes shimmering all bright and beautiful, her hand on his chest closing over his medallion.

He swept in and kissed her, parted her lips with his tongue and when she opened for him, he delved deeper into the recesses of her mouth and sighed with complete pleasure as he tasted her with a long swipe of his tongue across her tongue.

"Oh my." A gasp against his lips.

"Come closer." He locked his arms around her and kissed her with helpless yearning, his cock hardening and pressing against the front flap of his finely-made breeches. He thirsted for even more of her luscious mouth. He kissed her passionately, completely, drawing in her exquisite essence.

She arched her back, her mouth clinging to his as she pressed her breasts against his chest. "This is wonderful."

"Blissfully wonderful." He made love to her mouth,

using all the skills he had in his arsenal. He never wanted her to forget this moment, nor for him to forget it either. Flooded with a wealth of intense emotions and sensations, he fed on her as if she were the finest wine. She quite likely was. He'd never tasted anything more divine.

"This. Us." She dug her fingers into his shoulders. "Tell me this is real."

"It's real." He grasped her bottom, lifted and seated her on the windowsill, which afforded him the chance to get even closer. Cupping her breasts below the neckline of her gown, he lifted her bosom higher until the upper pink of her nipples showed, then he dipped in and buried his face in her creamy mounds. With a ravenous growl, he muttered, "You've no idea how much I've wanted to touch you like this."

"Really?" With one hand under his chin, she lifted his gaze back to hers, then slowly, gently, she caressed his lower lip with her fingers. "Your kisses are divine."

He stuck his face in her neck, kissed her soft skin, her enticing orange blossom fragrance wafting around him. "You truly are an angel, *Amore*. A wonderful kisser."

"I currently have a wonderful teacher. Will you show me what else there can be between two people?"

"You are asking for trouble." Although he stroked her breasts, her nipples beading underneath the white lace of her gown. "We need to stop."

"No one has ever made me feel the way you do."

"Any man could make you feel like this, provided he knew what he was doing." He captured her mouth again, their kiss going on and on, growing rougher as he plundered and explored her mouth to his heart's content.

When he finally pulled back, he looked deep into her eyes. "I could kiss your luscious mouth all night long."

Breathlessly, she leaned back against the window frame, one hand fluttering over her gold locket. "I could easily allow it."

"Cease encouraging me. I've acted like a rake tonight."

"What of me? I'm the one who asked you to kiss me."

"You are an innocent lady, will always be so." He gripped her hips, lifted her from the windowsill and set her slippered feet back on the carpet.

"Do you truly prefer bachelorhood? You'll never change your mind about taking a wife in truth?" The look in her eyes begged him to say otherwise.

"I'm sorry." A shake of his head. "I will never marry."

Chapter 8

The next morning Olivia awoke in muddled disbelief, as if she was still half asleep. She curled onto her side, one hand tucked under her cheek, her pillow a soft haven of warmth and the invitation Anteros had handed her lying atop her bedside table, the parchment proof that last night hadn't been a dream at all, nor his divine kisses. She would soon be sailing on board Anteros's ship to the Mediterranean, to attend a ball being held at the Royal Palace of Palermo, to speak marriage vows with him, false marriage vows of course, but still, what a journey of excitement she had ahead of her.

A knock at her door, her maid calling out, "My lady. May I enter?"

"Yes, do come in." She sat up, propped her pillow behind her back and smiled as Lucy bustled inside and placed her morning breakfast tray on the table near her window. Her maid swept her floral pink and yellow drapes open before glancing to the gardens below. "It's windy outside today."

"Is it?" From her position in bed, she lifted her chin to get a better look. The sky held bands of gray cloud streaked by the wind. The heavy boughs of the trees swayed, and the brisk breeze sent fallen leaves skittering across the lawn.

"There might be a shower or two later this afternoon. Do you still wish to ride?" Lucy collected her peach-colored dressing gown and returned to her bedside.

"Yes, most certainly." A strong wind had never deterred her from a ride. "Miss Adrestia Bourbon and Captain Bourbon will be here at ten." She thrust her cherry-colored covers back and swung out of bed, pushed her arms into the sleeves of her robe and tied the sash around her waist. "I'll wear my royal-blue riding habit. It has woolen skirts and will keep me warm no matter how vigorous the wind gets."

Barefoot, she padded to her side table, eased into her chair and stirred sugar into her tea. A dash of milk too, then she sipped the sweet brew and breathed deep of the hearty aroma of the freshly buttered bread rolls still warm from the ovens. A slather of marmalade and her mouth watered as she bit into the light and airy softness of the bread, the preserve so sweetly delicious atop.

Lucy foraged inside her wardrobe, emerged and draped her riding habit on her bed, then collected her gloves and riding boots before swishing to the door. "I'll have your mare readied for your ride, then return to aid you in dressing."

"You are a treasure. Thank you, Lucy."

Her maid closed the door behind her.

After licking a drop of marmalade from one finger, she

opened her window a notch and breathed in the slight dampness in the air. Birds chirped from their treetop nests and water splashed in the garden fountain far below.

Another knock and Mama tottered in with a large bouquet of flowers overflowing her arms, the arrangement holding elegant golden-yellow roses, aromatic lilies, crimson-colored germini, and an abundance of white jasmine.

"These just arrived for you." Mama set the vase on the table, dropped a kiss on the top of her head then seated herself, her golden hair wisped with streaks of silver coiled high upon her head.

"They're beautiful." She searched the flowers and found a sealed card poking out from the fragrant blooms, the insignia embedded in the red wax belonging to Anteros. Gently, she caressed the smooth curls of the cobra's body and head emblazoned upon the seal. "The flowers are from the captain."

"Well, you two did spend a great deal of time together at the ball last eve. I'm not surprised he sent you flowers today."

"We are friends, Mama." She unfolded the small card. "Nothing more."

"No, my child, there is far more to your relationship with the captain than mere friendship alone. A mother can tell. Anteros Bourbon guards you like a hawk. He always does whenever he's in town." A fluff of Mama's navy skirts as she crossed her legs, her glittering silver wrap a beautiful contrast of color as it skimmed her shoulders. "Do you wish for more with him?"

"Yes." That single word slipped from her lips with

such hope infusing it. "Unfortunately, he never intends on taking a wife. He believes he lives a dangerous life, one he doesn't wish to entangle a wife within."

"That might be what he says, but he looks at you and sees the future he desires."

"That doesn't change the truth though, or his intentions."

"My dear, I believe you need some motherly advice."

"Go right ahead." She ate another bite of her bread roll.

"Follow your heart, my child, just as I followed mine when I allowed your papa to guard me like a hawk." An audacious wink, although not unsurprising. Mama could be shockingly audacious at times.

"I see," she murmured as she propped one elbow on the table, rested her chin in her open palm. "What if I told you that last eve my hawk handed me an invitation to a ball at the Royal Palace of Palermo?"

Mama's mouth gaped open. "As in Palermo, Sicily?"

"Yes. Adrestia received an invitation too, directly from Maria Cristina, the Duchess of Genoa who is currently residing in the palace with her parents. The ball is being held in the duchess's honor, and Anteros has offered me safe passage aboard his ship to attend the event."

"How on earth—I mean—oh my." Mama fluttered a hand over her chest. "You must go, Olivia. You can't turn down such an esteemed invitation, not from the Duchess of Genoa."

"Will you come with me?" She already knew Mama's answer, but she asked nonetheless.

"Oh, sweet child of mine, you know I suffer from such

terrible seasickness whenever I'm on the water. I won't be able to chaperone you on board the ship, although provided you take Lucy and a footman who can serve as a guard, then I'll be content and assured of your safety. I trust the captain. He would never allow any harm to come to you. Adrestia will be with you as well, correct?"

"She will. You truly don't mind that I'll be gone for a little while?"

"Not at all. You have been most fortunate to have been asked. You must go."

"Thank you, Mama. I'm so excited about this trip and all the new places I'll get to see."

"You'll have a wonderful time, I'm sure of it." Mama pointed to the card. "Read it to me. I must know what Anteros has written."

Smiling, she unfolded the card and read Anteros's elegantly written hand.

"My enchanting Olivia,

Please accept these flowers as a token of our friendship. They are as radiant as the angel I have sent them to. Adrestia and I shall see you at ten for our ride in the park. Dress warmly. It appears there is a fierce wind today.

Yours,
Anteros."

"Ten o'clock is fast approaching." Mama rose and squeezed her hand. "I shan't keep you, not when I have errands to run in town." With a jaunty wave, Mama swished out the door.

Yes, she must ready herself. Lucy wouldn't be far away. She tossed her robe and ivory nightgown on her bed then slipped on a chemise and cream blouse which she buttoned at the front, the neckline ruffled with layers that fluffed under her chin, her locket hidden underneath the fabric where it lay warm against her skin. Stockings and royal-blue skirts next, then she sat at her dressing table just as Lucy reappeared.

"My apologies, my lady. I got held up trying to find one of the groomsmen to saddle your mare. How would you like your hair arranged?"

"I'd like it left down today please." Over her shoulder, she handed Lucy her brush, the breeze slipping through her window swirling the sweet fragrance of the blooms from her beautiful bouquet. Her maid brushed her hair until the mass of thick golden curls bobbed in a glittering fall down her back.

Done, she rose from her chair, slipped her arms into her riding jacket and buttoned it. Boots laced and gloves tugged on, she nabbed her royal-blue hat, selected a golden-yellow rose from the bouquet and pinned it to her jacket as she walked from her chamber.

Along the top landing, she caught voices echoing to her from below in the front foyer. She grasped the railing and leaned over. Looking glorious in a forest-green riding jacket and skirt embroidered with swirling golden leaves, Adrestia stood below with their butler, a dainty forest-green hat pinned atop her head.

She must have made a noise since Adrestia lifted her gaze and smiled. "There you are. Jeeves let me in."

"I'm coming." She skipped downstairs as Jeeves

disappeared down the hallway, leaving them alone. She bounced off the bottom step and hugged Adrestia. "How are you today?"

"Invigorated and ready for a ride. Oh, and before I forget, Anteros asked the chef to pack us a picnic lunch to enjoy at the park, our usual spot in the wooded clearing next to the lake. One of our footmen loaded the picnic basket in the curricle and has already gone on ahead of us to set it up." Adrestia squeezed her back, whispered in her ear, "Anteros also told me you've accepted his proposal. When I heard of his plan to foil Father by speaking false marriage vows with you, I knew there wasn't a chance you'd ever turn his request down. We shall have such a wonderful trip to Sicily, and I promise Anteros and I will show you as many of our favorite places as we can along the way. The Duchess of Genoa's ball will be a stunning event to attend."

"Mama's already given me her approval to sail with both of you, although I didn't mention the proposal of course. It's best I keep all of that from her, otherwise she will only worry unnecessarily." A whispered answer in Adrestia's ear, their conversation going no farther than the two of them.

"I won't speak a word about it to her either."

Bootsteps crunched the gravel and Anteros stepped inside. Dressed in tight-fitting tan breeches which hugged his strong thighs, his riding boots buckled just below his knees and his sapphire blue jacket showing off the breadth of his broad shoulders, he appeared incredibly handsome. Even more so as he pressed one hand behind his back and offered her a deep bow, his neckcloth knotted and tailcoats swaying. "Good morning, Lady Olivia. You look as radiant as always."

"Sir, thank you for the flowers. They're beautiful." Her heartbeat fluttered all over the place, not keeping any proper rhythm at all, and her thoughts, oh my, they swiftly veered back to the time when she'd been in his arms last night.

"You're most welcome." A glance at the rose pinned to her jacket, then a playful smile as he caught her gloved hand and pressed a kiss to her knuckles. "I picked the flowers myself from my garden."

"You have a garden?" She'd never seen one when visiting his home in the past, other than for the flower boxes adorning the short pathway leading up to his front door. No roses or lilies were planted there though.

"I recently acquired the residence which sits on the street directly behind my home. It has extensive gardens which I raided this morning."

"You mean Grace Hall?" It abutted his, although no one had lived there for several months.

"Yes, I do. I've taken the boundary fence between my property and the Hall down, so now I have a rather large rear garden. The Hall will need upgrading and refurbishing since the previous owners neglected it these past few years, but once the work is completed, it'll be a wonderful addition to my property portfolio."

"Cease waffling on about your gardens and property portfolio. We're eager to be away, *Fratello*." Adrestia swished out the door, calling over her shoulder. "It's time to ride."

"Did you speak to your mama about our forthcoming

trip?" He offered his arm and she accepted. They stepped outside and walked along the path toward the driveway.

"Yes, and Mama was excited to hear about the invitation to the ball at Palermo, which she quickly insisted I must attend. That is all she's aware of though. I'd like to keep it that way."

"You have my agreement on that front." Across the other side of the driveway, their head groomsman cupped his palms and aided Adrestia atop her mount, while Sawman, the groomsman's son who also served as a guard when she rode, brought her mare forward from the stables. Anteros accepted the reins and waved Sawman away, then keeping her horse between them and the others, he dipped his head closer, his warm breath fluttering a few loose strands of hair across her cheek. "I'll show you my new rear gardens later today."

"You will?"

"I always keep a promise once it's made." He snuck her riding hat from her hand, set it atop her head and laced the ribbons underneath her chin. "I dreamed of you last night. All night. Of having you in my arms and kissing you again."

"You did?" She swayed.

"I've more pirate tendencies than a gentleman's, I'm afraid." A chuckle as he clasped her waist and lifted her into her saddle. He handed her mare's reins to her before mounting his own horse.

"Unfortunately, I like those pirate tendencies." A cheeky, sparring answer in return. She pressed her knees into her mount's sides and trotted in beside Adrestia, while Anteros came in on her other side. Together the three of them rode down the driveway and turned onto the street, Sawman atop his horse a short distance behind.

They clopped along, the wind rising and plastering her woolen skirts to her legs. A bird soared overhead, flying higher and higher, while a ginger-haired cat dashed across the street in front of them and skittered up a tree. Large hedges and front gardens lined each side of the road, stately homes hidden behind the lush greenery.

"*Mi piace sparring con te.*" Anteros doffed his hat toward her.

"Pardon?"

Adrestia bobbed in her saddle, the gait of her mare smooth as they trotted. "He said he enjoys sparring with you, *Sorella.*"

"Well, that has been obvious since the beginning." She arched a brow at him, although he looked ahead and whistled a merry tune.

They rode on, reaching a busier stretch as they entered the shopping area.

Peddlers hawked their wares from carts and a newspaper boy called out to passersby from one street corner.

Anteros continued his whistling, a different melody this time, not one she'd heard before.

"Are there lyrics to the tune you're whistling?" she asked.

"There are, but only in Sicilian. The lyrics talk of the blue tranquil waters of our homeland." A tip of his hat to two ladies strolling along the pathway.

"How different is Sicilian to Italian?" How he kept track of all the languages he spoke, she had no idea.

"There's a marked difference. Sicilian contains a medley of languages, with Greek, Hebrew, and Arabian words mixed in."

"How interesting." She longed to know more.

"There's also a difference between the tone and the structure of the sentences," Adrestia added. "If you wish to learn both languages, begin with Italian first, then delve into Sicilian."

"Would you tutor me?" She reached across the short gap between her and Adrestia, squeezed her gloved hand. "We'll have time while at sea, won't we?"

"If you sail with me on board The Decadence, then yes."

"Then I'll sail with you."

"You're sailing with me on The Cobra." Firm words from Anteros as he glanced behind him and searched among the hacks and carriages for someone or something. Only Sawman followed though.

"Are you looking for Giovani?" she checked.

"No, Giovani has gone on ahead to the park at my request. I asked him to hire a skiff from the lake vendors along the Serpentine, so we can enjoy a sail later. I'm looking for Bruno." One hard grunt. "He tailed us on our ride to your home so he won't be far away."

"Why can't I sail to Paradiso with Adrestia?" she asked, returning to their previous conversation. "She has agreed to teach me Italian."

"So did I last eve."

"Not words that I can repeat to another." She wagged a finger at him. "Did I mention that Lord Herbarth serenaded me with a merry tune once?" she added smartly, hopeful she could cajole him into singing the Sicilian tune. She truly wanted to hear it.

"Oooh, you are tugging on the tail of *the cobra*." A giggle from Adrestia. "Be careful, for *the cobra* can bite."

"Handsome Lord Herbarth." She released a soft sigh and what she hoped was a dreamy gaze to the streaky gray skies overhead. "He has such an entrancing voice, so easy to listen to. It's a gift being able to sing so well." She winked at Adrestia. "What is the Italian word for 'beloved?'"

"*Amati*."

"*Amati*," she repeated before arching a brow at Anteros. "Would you sing to me the words of your Sicilian tune, *Amati*?"

"You wish to compare my singing voice to that of your baron's?"

"Oh, there could surely be no comparison. Did I mention how entrancing his voice was?"

Adrestia burst into laughter. "Oh my, she spars better with each minute that passes. Sing the tune, *Fratello*."

"Don't encourage my bride-to-be." A mutter and dark look from Anteros.

Another laugh then Adrestia gestured to the arched entranceway into Hyde Park which appeared up ahead. "Let's have some fun. A race. First to our usual spot on the lake wins the rights to brag of their success for a week."

"Wait." She held a hand up. "Anteros's horse has thoroughbred blood. He needs to give you and I both a head start."

"Yes, I agree." A nod from Adrestia.

"Good." Without waiting another moment, Olivia

thrust her knees into her mare's sides and burst into a gallop, the wind rushing by as she tore under the arch. Across the royal parkland, she raced, hundreds of acres of hunting ground spread out before her, the grass green and lush with towering trees and the glistening waters of the Serpentine weaving through it all. Keeping her head tucked close to her horse's neck, she bolted as horses' hooves pounded close behind.

Anteros caught up to her first, his sapphire eyes bright and his hat now tucked under one arm so it didn't fly off, a mischievous look on his face. "Mind the dirt flying from my stallion's hooves, won't you?"

"How about you mind the dirt flying from mine?" With the silk ties of her pretty hat fluttering under her chin, she touched her cheek to her mount's neck and whispered, "Let's fly, girl."

Her mare snorted, nostrils flaring, her sleek brown coat gleaming, then she was off, weaving in and around the trees as the copse thickened.

Anteros thundered alongside her, Adrestia catching up then spurring ahead before splitting away as she followed the quickest route through the forest nearest the water's edge. Hers and Adrestia's mounts were so well matched in speed and endurance, although her friend's competitive streak had always been strong and Adrestia grinned before disappearing around the tight corner into the thickening woods.

No, she couldn't allow Adrestia to win this race, otherwise she'd never hear the end of it, not just for a week, but likely for a whole month. Following the same route, she made chase, splashing through muddy puddles and—

Her horse skidded and she went flying from her saddle.

Anteros plucked her from the air, slowed his mount and dropped her into his lap. With his arms bound tightly around her, his breathing rough, he muttered, "Are you hurt?"

"No, and that was a marvelous catch."

"A gentleman never allows his lady to get too far away from him, even when racing. I would have stayed by your side the entire time, in case you weren't aware." He dismounted, allowing her to slide into his saddle, then he stuffed his hat in his saddlebags before grasping her mare's dangling reins and calming her horse with a soft whisper in her ear. Gently, he ran his hands over her horse's legs, checking each one meticulously for any injury then done, he glanced at her. "She's fine, *mio angelo*, although my heart might never beat the same way again after seeing you tossed at such a fast speed. Are you certain you have no injuries?"

"Most certain, and I'm sorry." Needing to reassure him, she held out her arms and he caught her as she slid from his saddle, her feet hovering an inch or two above the ground as he held her against him. She embraced his strength, asked softly, "What is the Italian word for 'hero?'"

"*Eroe*." Huskily spoken as he rubbed his nose against her nose.

"And for 'kiss me?'"

"*Baciami*?" He looked deep into her eyes. "We are getting too close."

"Perhaps, or perhaps not close enough." Glad that

she'd lost Sawman during the race, she pushed her fingers into his silky black hair and stroked his scalp. "Thank you for being my *eroe*."

"Say the rest," he demanded. "I want you to."

"*Baciami*?" she whispered, then caught her breath as his eyes darkened with passion, his gaze lowering to her lips.

"Is everything all right?" A man appeared atop a horse, his dark coat flapping over the rump of his mount, a jagged scar bisecting one side of his face. The man who'd interrupted them last night. Signore Piero Bruno.

"Everything is fine. You though, have the worst timing." With a low growl, Anteros lifted her back into his saddle and mounted up behind her. A glance back at the man, along with a huff. "Bruno, allow me to introduce Lady Olivia Trentbury. My lady, meet Signore Piero Bruno, my father's man."

"My lady, I apologize for my intrusion during your conversation with the captain in the library last eve. I took my duty to his father a little too far." Bruno dipped his head, his eyes so black in color she couldn't even make out the difference between his irises and pupils.

"Apology accepted."

"Bruno, bring Lady Olivia's horse with you." Anteros nudged his stallion into a gentle trot, leaving Bruno behind.

"You don't like him, do you?" She wriggled to get a better look over his shoulder at the spy.

"There are no polite words to describe Bruno. Meanwhile you"—he caught an errant lock of her hair and twirled it around one finger, intrigue burning in his expressive eyes—"are beyond enchanting."

"Not only did Mama give me her blessing to travel to Sicily, but she also tossed some helpful advice in too." She pressed her lips to his ear and blew a soft breath against his lobe.

"Which was…"

"To follow my heart, just as she followed hers with Papa." She stroked along his firm jaw. "I miss him so much. He was honorable and loving, and I hope when I do eventually marry, it will be to a man exactly like him."

"Tell me more about your papa."

"His love for Mama and my brothers and sisters was so great, that even years later, his light still shines all around us. We miss him greatly of course, but our grief has eased over the years and now only wonderful memories of him arise when we think of him." Although sharing what she had about Papa with him brought tears to her eyes. She blinked and pushed those tears away. "My apologies."

"Don't ever fear showing your emotions around me." He tucked her head against his shoulder, murmured over the top of her head. "You bring forth in me the fierce desire to protect you."

"You do the same with me." She wriggled in his lap, something very large suddenly poking her in the bottom. Another wriggle and when he groaned, she gasped. "Are you all right?"

"Please, remain very still." He weaved through the thickening trees, so dense now she could no longer spot Bruno behind them. Goodness knows where Sawman had gotten to. Another poke. Another groan from him.

"What is that?" She wriggled some more.

"It is at times like these that I am reminded of exactly

how innocent you truly are, and of how unsuitable I am for you." He flicked open the top two buttons of her royal-blue jacket, hooked one finger underneath the ruffles at her neck and lifted her locket free before settling it where he could see it. Dipping his head to the pounding pulse point in her neck, he sucked the skin deep into his mouth.

"Anteros?" She leaned her head back. "That feels wonderful."

He released her skin with a soft pop, caught her hand and lowered it to his crotch, right over the thing currently poking her. "This is my cock, or you could call it a penis. It is a man's appendage, and when stirred to life it hardens and rises." He spread her fingers fully around the bulge. "My cock currently hungers for something which an innocent lady like you should never allow it to hunger for."

"It's incredibly firm and thick and long."

A devilish lift of his lips. "It feels agonizingly good when you touch me there." He glided her hand up and down his covered length and sweet heaven, he lengthened and thickened even further. "When a man gets as hard as I presently am," he continued with a throaty moan, "he will wish to push his cock between your legs and take you in the way only a husband should with his wife."

"Oh, I see." Eyes going wide, she lifted her hand free of his manhood. "How enlightening."

"Have I frightened you?"

"Did you wish to frighten me?"

"I wished to inform you of exactly how far you test my patience. If you want an affair, I'm your man, but if you want marriage, then you must look elsewhere." He guided his horse along the forested pathway, its hooves crunching pine needles and leaves, the wind rising with a howl as it swept through the swaying boughs overhead.

"I trust you, Anteros."

"I know you do." A caress of his hand along the lower curve of her back, his gaze sweeping down her neck and over the upper swells of her breasts. Desire. Need. Want. It all flared in his eyes as he lifted his gaze back to hers. "*Amore*, you tempt me beyond my endurance."

Her cheeks heated, her nipples hardening into tight peaks, while warmth pooled in her middle then dropped to center firmly between her thighs. "You tempt me beyond mine too."

He jerked his horse to a halt, muttered, "I can hear Adrestia. Our spot along the lake is directly through those trees. I need a moment alone, to calm my cock."

"I'll walk. Let me down." She'd aid him however she could.

"Thank you." He swung one leg over and dismounted, his booted feet thumping the ground, then he lifted her down and let her go.

She dashed through the trees, not wanting to leave him, but doing so all the same.

Chapter 9

The moment Anteros was back in Olivia's company, he had taken liberties with her that he shouldn't have. Right now all he wanted to do was make chase after her, to take her in his arms and kiss her again, exactly as he'd longed to do since their time together in the library had ended last eve. She was such a temptation, his angel a woman he desperately desired an affair with.

Slowly, he got his cock back under better control, just as Bruno joined him with Olivia's horse. He accepted the reins of her mount, grudgingly thanked the man and walked into the clearing by the lake, Bruno remaining at the verge of the woods.

Dainty yellow buttercups bobbed their heads within the lush grass, the trees surrounding the meadow forming a perfect half circle up to the edge of the lake, the reflection of the forest shimmering within the swell of the water.

Adrestia and Olivia stood at the shoreline, both ladies waving to Giovani as he sailed a skiff toward their private spot by the lakefront. Even after only a couple of days back on land, the choppy waves and brisk winds provided an incredible lure for him. A sail along the Serpentine later this afternoon would help ease that longing deep within his blood.

Leading his and Olivia's horses to the tree where his sister's mount grazed, he passed by the picnic his footman had laid out on a dark green and white tartan blanket, cutlery and glasses set next to the covered dishes which held his chef's wonderful fare. A pounding of hooves and Sawman emerged from the trees looking a whole lot flustered.

After securing the horses to a low branch, Anteros continued on toward the ladies.

Olivia faced the lakefront, her royal-blue habit's skirts collecting sand along the hem from the sandy shore in front, the short train at the back flaring across the grassy verge behind her. She had a beautiful hourglass figure, her waist tapering in, then the sweet curve of her hips arching out. She enticed him beyond measure, his fingers itching to strip her bare. If they were all alone, he might already have toppled her to the grass so he could roll around with her.

Such a ruthless need, a craving that wouldn't be sated until he'd had her. He was sure of it. Hell, he would pleasure her well if she allowed his touch.

Olivia hooked an arm through Adrestia's arm, tipped her gaze to the skies, the wind caressing her face. "Mmm, I can't believe I'll soon be sailing to the Mediterranean. Someone needs to pinch me so I know this is all real."

"It's real," he answered as he stepped in beside her, his hands stuffed in his pockets so he didn't actually pinch her.

He'd nip her bottom if he could.

"Captain!" A shout from Giovani as his man lowered the sail, skimmed the waves and bounded into the knee-deep water. Giovani grabbed the bow, dragged the skiff up onto the sand and slapped him on the back as he joined him. "I've hired this skiff for the remainder of the day. It's all yours when you wish for a sail."

"You have my thanks."

Giovani offered the ladies an elegant bow. "Good morning, ladies, or I should say good afternoon since it's now after midday. I'm famished and fairly certain I can smell chicken pie."

"Me too. Let's see what's under those silver domes." Adrestia curved her hand through Giovani's arm and the two led the way to the picnic spread out under the dappled shade of an elm tree.

"May I escort you to the picnic?" He extended his arm to Olivia.

"You certainly may." She accepted his arm and they strolled across.

His sister sank down on one of the two blankets, Giovani dropping in beside her. A lift of the domes covering the dishes and Adrestia clapped. "Oh my, our chef has delivered all of my favorites. Warm chicken pie, ham and cheese sandwiches, and scotch eggs. I'll serve the pie. Everyone, help yourselves to the sandwiches and eggs."

Giovani patted his rumbling stomach as he accepted a plate of pie from Adrestia. He dove into it and mumbled his appreciation around a huge mouthful.

"Where are your manners, Giovani?" Still standing, Olivia laughed as she unbuttoned her royal-blue riding jacket and folded it. "You're not supposed to eat before all the ladies are seated."

"*Mie scuse.*" He stuffed more pie into his mouth. "Hurry and sit so I don't appear so atrociously unpolite."

Another laugh as Olivia seated herself on the blanket and dropped her folded jacket on the grass behind her. A fluff of her long skirts as she ensured she covered her ankles, then she tugged off her gloves and released the ribbons holding her blue riding hat in place, her hair shimmering with soft and bright shades of gold down her back. A pat of the space next to her. "There's plenty of room. Come and sit beside me, *Amati.*"

"You need only ask me once." He sprawled out beside her, and needing to touch her, lifted one of her long curls and allowed the golden strands to slip through his fingers. "*Il mio bellissimo angelo*, feed me."

"Pie first?" She sent him a veiled look through her lowered lashes.

"Yes," he whispered in her ear as he tried hard to keep from sliding one hand around her nape and drawing her mouth to his. No more than three inches separated them and he wished there were far less.

She glanced at Adrestia and Giovani who chatted quietly to each other as they ate, then she placed a plate of pie holding two slices between them on the blanket. Cutlery in hand, she cut into it and held the first forkful to his mouth. When he opened, she slid the morsel between his lips and he chewed while she forked a bite for herself. She slapped her lips together over the fork and moaned her delight.

The most wicked moan he'd ever heard. One that did

strange things to his heart.

Damnation, but he liked watching her eat, how she closed her eyes for just a moment so she could savor the taste, then how she opened her eyes and licked her lips once she'd swallowed. Mmm, he wanted to capture her mouth and eat her rather than the pie.

"Do you want some more?" she murmured as she dangled another forkful in front of his mouth.

"*Per favore.*" He wrapped his hand around her fingers and clamped his mouth down on the fork.

She giggled, tugged her fingers free and ate some more pie. "You and Giovani have the same terrible manners."

"I have never professed to having any manners at all." He accepted another forkful which she held out for him. "Are you enjoying your afternoon?" he asked after he swallowed.

"Yes, immensely. I'm feeling very fortunate too. I'm here with close friends, enjoying wonderful food and making new memories. There is nothing I enjoy more." She leaned in, brushed a crumb from his chin then continued in a whisper, "You appear more relaxed now. I like this unrestrained side of you."

"You wouldn't if you realized how very close I am to pouncing on you."

"Manners, sir." Smiling, she tapped his nose, then she selected a scotch egg, her gaze going to the water and suddenly becoming rather pensive. "I don't think I've ever told you, but my papa used to bring me to this lake all the time when I was a child. He'd hire a skiff as you've done today, then he'd sail us along the length of the Serpentine. We'd stop somewhere along the shoreline, eat sandwiches and feed the birds. I remember each and every outing as if it were yesterday."

"I wish I could have met him." He touched the back of one hand to her soft cheek.

"I wish you could've too." She remained perfectly still, a vulnerable look filling her eyes, her voice lowered as she whispered, "Do you believe it's possible for us to belong to someone, from the day we first meet them?"

"Pardon?"

"I mean, my parents did. They loved each other from the very beginning. Do you think my question an unusual one?"

"Yes, and belonging to someone, well, that all sounds rather fanciful to me."

"Which means you don't believe it's possible." A sad statement. She went quiet as she glanced out over the water again. A long minute passed before she looked at him once more and when she did, her gaze snagged on the medallion holding his cobra insignia. "How did you come by that precious piece?"

"That is quite the story. I was young, still a boy at the time when I found it." A story he'd never shared with anyone, other than Adrestia and Giovani.

"Please, tell me the story." The look of longing in her eyes…

…hell, it melted his resolve. "Ten, I was at the time."

"Keep going," she urged when he stopped for a second.

"I used to spend many afternoons exploring the underground tunnels of my grandfather's archeological site on Paradiso."

"Your paternal or maternal grandfather?"

"Ah, well interestingly, the man I called my grandfather was in fact my godfather, a close relative on my father's side, so paternal. One day when I was deep within Grandfather's tunnels, I came across a small slit in the rock wall which opened up two or three feet farther in. At the time Grandfather had commissioned an engineering professor to aid him in building a pulley system so he could hoist the ancient artifacts from deep within the ruins up to the surface. His desire was to preserve the artifacts for future generations. The professor's seven-year-old daughter was with me when I discovered the slit. Over the next few weeks, she and I managed to chip away at the rock wall until we'd finally gotten that slit wide enough so I could edge my scrawny body through. A small cavern opened up from that slit, rocks and dust everywhere, as well as my medallion hooked on a crevice. Someone must have tossed it through the slit, the piece lost for centuries until I claimed it as mine." When he'd first placed the gold chain with the emblem of the cobra around his neck, the medallion had settled against his chest and a strange warmth had infused him. A feeling of rightness had bloomed, never once receding, not in all these years.

"It is the perfect insignia for you, particularly when you snap and bite just like the cobra does when someone gets between you and those you hold dear to your heart. Thank you for sharing such a precious story with me. It means the world that you did. Are you still hungry?" she asked and at his nod, she placed a ham and cheese sandwich on his plate.

Their footman stepped forward from where he stood

several feet away and served the wine, then the four of them chatted, more stories and shared memories exchanged. He hadn't enjoyed such a relaxing time in ages.

With his belly full, he rested his head back on the blanket and closed his eyes, Adrestia, Giovani, and Olivia's continued conversation swirling around him. These three people were like an extension of himself, in many ways a crucial and necessary extension. Adrestia was just like him, but the feminine more loving version. She'd go into battle for those she held dear to her heart, just as he would. Giovani was a rock, always standing solidly at his side, a friend he'd shared every single adventure with since they'd met as children. Olivia was…well, she was something far more than anyone had ever been to him. She'd taken up a place in his heart and continued to gobble up more room with each day that passed.

Whenever he was away from her, he ached to see her again.

Whenever he was close to her, he ached to get even closer.

It seemed a vicious cycle he couldn't break.

"Are you sleeping?" She laid down next to him, her shoulder now brushing his shoulder.

"No, just resting my eyes." He snuck a look at her, surprised to see only the two of them on the blanket. Adrestia and Giovani now ambled along the shoreline, enjoying a short walk. A glance behind him showed Bruno no longer lingered at the edge of the woods. He'd disappeared somewhere, and Sawman sat with his back propped against a trunk as he whittled away at a piece of wood. Excellent, he had some freedom from Bruno.

Freedom he intended on claiming this very second.

He launched to his feet, extended both hands. "This is the perfect time for you and I to escape. We can enjoy a sail on the lake, just the two of us."

"Oh, surely Adrestia and Giovani should come with us. We need a suitable chaperone, particularly considering what happened earlier on your horse. Don't you agree?" She placed her hands in his and he tightened his grip and gently drew her to her feet.

"No, not when we can easily stay within sight of them and your guard." Perhaps he needed a sweetener to ensure her agreement. "If you come with me, just the two of us, I'll tell you exactly how and when and where I first met Giovani." Hearing him waffle on about his earlier years seemed to be what she desired most.

"Yes please, in that case, let's go." A beaming smile.

"Excellent." A chuckle as he guided her to the sand. He aided her into the skiff and once she was settled on the bench seat at the stern, he pushed the skiff into the shallows and waved to Adrestia and Giovani. "We'll be back soon."

"Take care," Adrestia called with a wave in return.

"Take your time," Giovani added with a smirk.

"Will do." He ignored that smirk, removed his sapphire blue riding jacket, folded it underneath the seat and got rid of his neckcloth. A flick of the top two buttons of his shirt so he could enjoy the breeze, then he collected the oars. From the center seat, he thrust the oars into the waves and sent them skimming out across the water, then once he'd passed the breakers, he tucked the oars away, gripped the ropes and raised the sail. The wind filled the canvas with a vigorous slap and with his booted feet braced wide along the side of the skiff, he steered them through the rougher swell. "Today is a perfect day to be out on the water."

"Look!" Olivia pointed to several fish jumping out and splashing back in. A seagull soared downward, wings tucked in. It plunged under the waves then emerged with a fish between its beaks and gobbled its meal. Laughing, she grasped her hair blowing in the wind, her locks long and loose without her hat to keep them contained. Half leaning over the side of the skiff, she giggled, her blouse plastered to her chest and the cream fabric showing the lacy outline of her chemise underneath. "Thank you for hiring a skiff. The Serpentine is beautiful and sailing along it is glorious."

"The sight before me is far more beautiful." He couldn't drag his gaze from hers.

"Papa always enjoyed hunting in this park. There are plentiful deer and other wild animals." She gestured to his white shirt now splotched with water. "You're getting wet."

"Such is the life when one is a sailor." The wind rushed past and the waves pounded against the bow, spraying even more water over him. "Do you want to come and help me hold the ropes?"

"Yes, please." Cheeks flushed a rosy color, she stood and swayed.

"Come quickly." He held out a hand and nabbed her around the waist, pulled her hard up against his chest. "Place your hands around mine on the ropes. I won't let go of either them or you."

She wriggled around, her back to his chest, her hands sliding over his hands. "I don't want to topple us overboard. I can't swim in these heavy woolen skirts. I'd have to—"

"Don't say—"

"—dispense of them."

"—it." Now all he could envision was her dressed in nothing but her blouse, that imagery sending a buzz of heat flaring at the base of his spine and searing around to his cock. With her bottom tucked nicely into his groin, his cock rose to the challenge of trying to get even closer.

"We're sailing out of sight of the others. I can't see Adrestia or Giovani any longer." She wriggled against his erection, her lower cheeks snug either side of his shaft. A gasp as she glanced over her shoulder at him. "Oh my, you seem to be getting no relief from your manhood today."

"At least no one can tell what we're doing or who we are this far from the shore." Keeping the ropes steady, his woman firm in the circle of his arms, he steered them across the swell of white-tipped waves.

"Papa never sailed in such strong winds as these, or with the skiff half out of the water as you've got it. If I reach over, I could almost touch the waves. I'm sure of it."

"Try it. Touch them."

"Are you certain?"

"Of course." He angled his body sideways to give her better access to the waves and she turned in his arms then skimmed her fingers through the white surf. A burst of delightful giggles had her breasts bumping up and down against his chest.

"This is an awe-inspiring experience." She faced him fully, cupped his right cheek, her gentle touch making his heartbeat race. "How did you first meet Giovani? You promised you'd tell me the tale."

"Giovani and I are the same age. He was a lad of eleven when he came to Paradiso Island from Naples with his father, a master winemaker. My grandfather hired his father to oversee our vineyards, including the production and bottling of the wine. Giovani and I forged a strong friendship from the very first day we met. We would go sailing around the island together, dive along the reefs, fish with spears. Those sorts of things. We both had the exact same love of the sea." Grasping the sail's rope with one hand, he spread his other hand more firmly over her hip, then stroked lower still, over the lush curves of her backside hidden underneath the heavy layers of her riding skirts. She wriggled her hips against his hips and blast it, his cock filled even further and pressed hard against her belly.

"Anteros." Her breathing came faster, his as well.

"I'm sorry, but my cock desperately wants to jab between your legs and settle itself in your heat."

"You shouldn't say such things to a lady." She twined her arms around his neck, pressed her cheek against his cheek and whispered in his ear, "*Baciami*?"

"You don't know what you're asking."

"I certainly—"

The skiff crested a huge wave, which came out of nowhere and he gripped the ropes tighter, his biceps tensing and every muscle straining as he worked to control the wind power he'd harnessed in the skiff's tight sail. "Hold tight," he yelled, the bow rising sharply upward.

The hull slammed down and water drenched them.

He grappled to keep his footing, Olivia clinging to him. A quick change of course to keep them upright and he sailed through the critical moment. "Are you all right?"

"I'm fine. W-what about you?" Olivia shivered, water dripping from her, his angel completely drenched.

"There's nothing quite like a wild wind to fill a sailor's heart with contentment."

"I should have expected that answer." She wiped her face with her wet sleeve. "I'll need to go home and change. I can't possibly return to the meadow like this."

"There will be hackneys for hire near the entrance to the park." Up ahead, boats for hire bobbed near the jutting wharf, the arched entrance to the park rising behind it. "We're almost there."

"Wonderful." A huge smile suddenly lifted her luscious lips. "I can't believe how happy I am right now, sopping wet and totally disheveled. I love water, no matter what form it comes in."

"So do I. We have so much common." As he neared the shoreline, he turned the skiff a touch more, enough for the wind not to hit the sail quite so fully, then holding her tight around her waist, he bounded back into the hull and aided her back onto the seat at the stern.

A grip of the rudder. He skimmed the waves toward the wharf, then he dropped the sail completely as he came in alongside the pier. He tossed a rope to the hire master and the man brought them in.

Snagging his jacket from under the seat, he wrung the water from it then swung it over Olivia's shoulders to hide her now see-through blouse as best as he could. Onto the dock, he bounded, reached back for her and aided her onto the wooden platform beside him.

Ushering her along the jetty, he raised a hand to hail

the closest hackney and the driver opened the door of his conveyance for him. He thanked the man and gave him instructions to take them directly to Grace Hall before handing Olivia inside into the warmth of the coach. In the darkened confines of the hackney, the curtains pulled across the windows, he removed his soggy jacket from her shoulders just as the hackney jerked forward and rattled through the arched gates onto the street.

"Since we both need to get changed and my home is far closer than yours, you can borrow whatever you'd like from Adrestia's wardrobe. She won't mind in the least." He certainly wasn't prepared to end his day with her, not yet, not in any way. "It'll be safer alighting from the hackney at Grace Hall rather than at the front door of my residence. We can easily sneak through the rear gardens to the servants' entrance. I did promise to show you those gardens today, and I never break a promise."

"Yes, that's a good plan." In her drenched skirts, her hair dripping and skin slick, she shivered and inched closer into his side.

"We can share body heat if you like?" He didn't wait for her agreement but lifted her from the squabs and settled her in his lap.

"Anteros." She gave a little shriek as she clutched his shoulders, her nipples pebbling tight and poking into the thin silk of her cream blouse. "You need to warn a lady before you do something like that."

"I'd rather not." His breeches tightened, the bulge at the front unmistakable. "I need to kiss you. That's all the warning you're going to get."

"That could be dangerous considering our current

location." Sliding one hand around the back of his head, she touched her nose to his nose, their breath melding as she scooted even closer.

"I thrive on danger. I believe you do too." He wanted her so badly, and it appeared she wanted him too. This connection between them wasn't going to dissipate on its own, nor his fierce hunger for her, not when she continued to torment him so. He captured her mouth and kissed her, traced his tongue across her tongue as he invaded her mouth. "Tell me to stop if I go too far," he muttered as he plundered between her lips.

"Don't stop. Please, don't stop." She wriggled in his lap.

"I want to devour you, Olivia." He sucked her bottom lip between his lips and bit gently on her soft flesh. She nipped his lower lip in return, and he couldn't hold back. He released a long stream of Italian, then allowed his raging need for her its full release and gave himself over to the heady passion roaring through him. Kissing her deeply, he ravished her mouth over and over, until her lips were delectably swollen and her heartbeat thumped madly against his own pounding heart.

No stopping now.

Chapter 10

Desire rushed through Olivia as Anteros wrapped her fully up in a wondrous spell of need. He urged her lips farther apart and plunged his tongue inside her mouth. His kisses were divine and held an edge of hunger she couldn't ignore, not when the same hunger roared through her as well. She pressed her breasts against his chest and embraced his heat, stroked down his sides, her shivers easing as he laid her down on the hackney's bench seat and settled himself over top of her. She roamed around to his back and down over his bottom encased in hip-hugging tan breeches, his buttocks tightening in her grasp and his shaft poking determinedly into her belly.

Heat flushed her cheeks at her brazen behavior.

She shouldn't be engaging in such a sensual romp with him, but then she had no choice. She'd fallen in love with him the very first day she'd met him, and it had become impossible to ignore her feelings any longer.

"Let me touch you the way I want to," he whispered

against her lips. "Say yes."

"Yes." Without question, she gave him her agreement.

A devasting smile as he slowly slipped the edge of her damp blouse and lacy undergarment over one shoulder and exposed her right breast. He moaned, dipped his head and grazed his teeth over her nipple and oh my, her need for him doubled.

"Do you like me kissing you here?" he murmured around her nipple.

"Yes."

"This is exactly why innocent ladies need a chaperone." He lifted his head, dropped a kiss on her locket before brushing his mouth over hers in a teasing caress.

"We are an engaged couple."

"Falsely engaged, and no one here in London will learn about that false engagement other than who we've already told." He grinned, rather wickedly. "You have beautiful breasts, *Amore*. I want to taste both of them."

"Wait." She yanked her blouse back over her shoulder and palmed his wet chest.

"No, we Bourbon men do not like it when our women cover themselves up." He snapped his teeth together and released a low growl.

"Before we go any further, we need to discuss this." She curled her fingers around his dangling medallion. "I need to know what's happening between us."

"I wish for an affair, one in which I promise I'll keep your virtue intact. I thirst for more, although I'll never take your maidenhead, not when it belongs to your future husband. Will you allow me to show you all the pleasure that's possible when a man and a woman come together?

We can take things slowly." He lowered his tone, his voice a seductive whisper between thcm. "I crave you."

"When you kissed me last eve, I came alive for the first time in my life. You belong to me, Anteros, and I belong to you. Maybe that is a fanciful notion to you, but it isn't to me." Maybe it would take some time for him to come around to her way of thinking, but she had time, particularly when they'd soon be sailing together to Sicily. "When you're away at sea, I count down the days until you return."

"Are you saying yes to an affair?" He touched her chin, kissed her lips.

"I long for more time with you." She certainly couldn't just turn her love for him off, as if it didn't exist. "Yes, I'm saying yes."

"I can't wait to get you into my bed." He tugged gently on her lower lip with his teeth, which sent delightful shivers coursing down her spine. She moaned and arched her back, and he nibbled on her upper lip next as he toyed with one of her damp curls.

"Grace Hall!" A call from the driver up top, then the hackney slowed and stopped.

"We'll resume this conversation once we're inside and changed." Anteros lifted his sapphire blue riding jacket back over her shoulders, then opened the door and aided her down onto the street, Grace Hall rising beyond the front trees and gardens.

He paid the driver, thanked him and sent him on his way. The hackney clattered down the street, the wind swirling and sending fallen leaves skittering in circles across the gravel driveway. Overhead, a heavy pall of gray clouds darkened to an ominous black and a crack of thunder boomed.

"Let's hurry. The heavens are about to open and unleash a downpour." With a hand at her back, he guided her into the seclusion of the grounds, along a hedged pathway then around to the rear of the residence, the Hall's windows cloaked and doors boarded up.

They weaved around a fishpond with lily pads and bright orange goldfish swimming about, rounded a corner then emerged before a central garden with a statue as its centerpiece. A beautiful statue. One of an angel with long locks and a cloth loosely draped over the angel's feminine body, the cloth hiding her breasts but not her midriff, concealing her hips and lower body but not her calves or bare feet. Her curved wings swept back, wingtips gracefully resting on the garden bed behind her.

In this quiet slice of paradise, she stepped closer and touched one golden-yellow rose bud blooming in front of the marble sculpture. Lilies bloomed to the left, crimson-colored germini to the right and an abundance of white jasmine were dotted all around. The wind swept through and swirled the luscious perfume of the flowers.

She smiled at Anteros. "These are the blooms from my bouquet. She's a beautiful angel, and this is an incredibly tranquil spot."

"She reminds me of you, *mio angelo*." He tugged his jacket more fully over her shoulders, the wind having blown one side away.

She didn't want to break their eye contact, nor this heavenly moment, not when the man before her filled her vision and her heart. "I want to experience passion at your hand." It was the truth, the utter truth. "There isn't anyone else I want to be with, other than you."

"I'm only offering an affair, nothing more." He plucked a golden-yellow rose from the bush, the bud tight and not yet fully open. Gently, he tucked the bloom behind her ear and kissed the tip of her nose.

"I've already said yes." She had no intention of changing her mind about the affair.

"I am going to take you to my bedchamber this second, light the fire and ensure you are warm, then we'll talk some more about the pleasure I intend on giving you."

"What about your staff?"

"My butler is very discreet. You can trust Bellini not to utter a word about your visit to another soul." He caught her hand, tugging her right along with him as he dashed around the garden. "The servants' entrance is this way."

Another rumble of thunder and raindrops splattered the ground.

Anteros opened the servants' door and steered her into a darkened lobby with two doors and a stairwell leading from it, the clatter of pots and pans echoing from behind the closest of the two doors.

"The kitchens?" she asked quietly.

"Yes." He drew her up the winding stairwell, oil burning in an iron wall sconce on the corner up ahead. They rounded the bend and when they reached the very top landing, he rubbed her arms to instill some warmth into her. "Wait here while I check the hallway remains clear."

She nodded, and he left through the door.

When he returned with a candle in hand, he snagged her around the waist and marched her along a passageway holding a thick burgundy and gold woven runner, the walls lined in a deep wine-colored silk wallpaper. Under a gilt-edged plaster arch, he guided her directly into a large bedchamber. His.

She now stood in Captain Anteros Bourbon's private rooms.

Rich sapphire covers with a golden cobra emblazoned across it graced a monstrous four-poster bed with a matching sapphire canopy sweeping down each of the carved posts. A wide bay window overlooked the gardens they'd just traversed, while heavy damask curtains of the same sapphire and gold color fell in an elegant drape to the cream carpeted floor. With the skies darkening outside, only the barest trace of light now filtering through, it appeared as if the night had fallen, the day completely at an end.

Anteros closed the door with a quiet click, strode to the fireplace, crouched and lit the kindling arranged within the hearth. Flames took ahold and he added a stack of wood until the fire burned a fiery red-gold.

After setting the candle in a holder on his oak mantelpiece, he toed off his boots and beckoned with one finger. "Come closer."

She joined him, shrugged out of his jacket, the golden-yellow rose fluttering from her ear to the floor.

He lowered to one knee and unlaced her riding boots. "I want to be wicked with you, *Amore*. Do you want to be wicked with me?"

"I do."

"That is the perfect answer." He plucked her boots off, set them on the hearth then curled one hand around her calf and slid his fingers higher until he grasped her garter. He removed it, rolled her stocking down her leg and rubbed her chilled foot before reaching up for her other garter. Slowly, he drew her second stocking down and warmed her other foot between his hands.

Rising to his feet, he unbuttoned his white shirt, tossed it aside, his gold medallion swaying before it came to rest over his heart. Broad shoulders, and sun-kissed skin. Oh my. He must go shirtless on board his ship. Skimming lower, she gulped for a breath. His torso held twin roped muscles either side of his hips which speared downward and disappeared below the waistband of his tan rawhide breeches. A dagger glinted from a leather sheath at his wrist, his saber strapped to one hip.

"I love the way you look at me."

She tore her gaze from his half naked body back to his face.

"Do you want me to fetch a change of clothes from Adrestia's wardrobe now, or perhaps later?" He leaned over her, dropped a kiss on the top of her head.

"Now, please."

"Wait here. I won't be long." He left and closed the door behind him.

She stepped closer to the warmth of the fire where a painting hung above it, one of Anteros and Adrestia seated bareback atop horses on a white sand beach with a turreted castle rising behind them. Such a stunning piece of work, and rather recently painted considering Anteros and Adrestia looked around the same age as the portrait currently depicted.

She touched a finger to the battlements running

between two of the four corner towers, the distinct colors of Anteros's gold and sapphire cobra flag flying from the top of each tower. Built of thick slabs of tawny-colored stone, the castle stood three floors in height and sat on a blustery point with a bird's eye view of the sea before it. Waves splashed against one high rock wall and sprayed a rainbow of colors, the sky painted a mix of sunset yellows and oranges. In one lower corner the words *La Rocca Dinastia, Island of Paradiso, Sicily,* appeared in a neat flourish.

He owned this magnificent castle and the island on which it sat. Incredible.

Anteros was a man who'd established an empire and she wasn't sure exactly how he had, although she intended on uncovering every single thing about him, every secret included.

"I see the painting has caught your attention." The door shut with a soft click and he stood on the carpet with a red velvet gown folded over one arm, the hem embroidered with white lace. Bundled over his other arm was a chemise, stockings, matching red slippers, and a black hooded cloak.

"You've thought of everything."

"I didn't want to have to leave you again, so I brought everything you might need." He sauntered toward a wooden trunk flush against one wall and laid his armful down on the closed lid. With his damp midnight-black hair sweeping his shoulders, he strolled back to her.

She pointed to the painting. "Tell me about La Rocca Dinastia."

"The *castello* holds over four hundred rooms, has two grand courtyards, four towers, along with galleries on the upper floor which display some beautiful frescoes my grandfather and his father before him collected over the years."

"Are there dungeons in your *castello*?"

"Of course." A glint in his eye. "Every captain needs dungeons where he can stow his prisoners captured at sea."

"What kind of prisoners do you capture?"

"Men who aren't to be released until they've learnt their lesson."

"You own a castle, a fleet of ships, a gaming club, this large residence, Grace Hall. What else am I missing?" She faced him, searched his gaze. "I'm trying to understand exactly who you are, Captain Bourbon. How on earth did you come to accumulate so much property?"

"That is an interesting question." His shoulders suddenly stiffened. "You seem rather fixated on what I own."

"Perhaps learning of the finer details might help me understand you better."

"I sincerely doubt it."

"Try me." She threw the challenge out, and he stared at her, not biting at—

"As you wish. I also own a palazzo in Naples, a villa along the cliffs of Lisbon overlooking the Tagus River, and other various parcels of land here and there."

"I see." She gulped, shocked at his answer.

"I have secrets upon secrets, *mio angelo*, none of which I can currently share with you, possibly ever."

"You don't trust me to keep your secrets?"

"There are only two people whom I trust."

"Adrestia and Giovani," she offered up.

"*Sì*." He backed her up a step. "You are a lady

searching for a husband. Are you absolutely certain you want an affair knowing that husband can't be me?"

"I've waited a lifetime to meet a man like you, Anteros."

"If you want me, then you may have me, but only on my terms." With painstaking slowness, he lifted his hands and flicked open the buttons of her cream blouse. She held perfectly still as he did, as he completed the task and pushed the garment from her shoulders. "Your chemise has to go too." A husky demand. "Skirts first though."

Since she desired his trust, she had to take the first step and give him hers. She released the buttons at her waist and the heavy royal-blue fabric thumped to the floor in a wet heap.

"I want you." He traced along the lacy neckline of her knee-length chemise, then grazed down between her covered breasts to her waist.

"Remove your weapons." She stated her own demand.

"Yes, my lady." A grin as he unbuckled his sword belt and wrist dagger. He propped his weapons against his trunk, stuck one bare foot on the edge of the lid, lifted the hem of his breeches and unstrapped an ankle dagger. He returned to her, his arms outstretched. "I am completely unarmed and at your disposal."

"Will you show me where you like to be touched?"

"Trust me, wherever you choose to touch me, will please me." He caught her up in his arms, laid her down on his bed and settled himself over top of her. With his entire length pressed against hers, he released a sensual moan that started a pulse point fluttering in her below. "*Amore*, being this close to you is sheer heaven."

"I can't believe I'm going to be wicked with you."

"There is only us, so be as wicked as you desire." With his thumb, he caressed her upper lip then swept to the corner and stroked along her lower lip. "I must kiss you."

"Please, yes." He brushed his mouth across her mouth and she stopped breathing altogether. Then he angled his head and deepened their kiss, his lips soft and warm, tender and coaxing. She touched the tip of her tongue to the tip of his tongue and when she did, a heady wave of pleasure swamped her, a primal form of pleasure which had her instinctively urging his mouth open even farther so she could explore him as fully as she could.

Low sounds erupted from his mouth, his chest vibrating as he rubbed against her, then his kiss changed, becoming hotter and more needy, his tongue pushing deeper between her lips as he licked the inside of her mouth.

With their warm breaths mingling, she spread her palms over his wickedly firm chest muscles. Heat flared in her core and pulsed through her. Never had she opened her heart to another man before, but she had with him, the very first day they'd met. His crisp chest hair tickled her fingertips and slowly, she smoothed lower, over the rigid contours of his abs, then she delved around to his sides where those beautifully corded muscles arrowed down over his trim hips. She gripped his arms, his biceps iron-hard and rippling with muscle. "You are built like a warrior."

"*Sì*, your warrior. I love the way you touch me." He cupped her face, kissed her passionately and she fell, down and down and down into the silken web of desire he spun so effortlessly around her.

"You truly are a dangerous man." Intoxicated by him, she swished along the waistband of his breeches, her heartbeat pounding so loud in her ears.

"Ladies usually run far from me, not toward me as you do. They understand the danger that comes with being in my company." He tugged the front lacings of her chemise open, eased the loose neckline over one shoulder and lowered his head to her breast. Fastening his hot mouth over her beaded nipple, he moaned against her skin and such a fierce explosion of sensation rippled through her.

She seized his shoulders and held on as he sent her world spinning. "Anteros?"

"I need to touch more of you, Olivia." Mouth suctioned over her nipple, he flicked the tip with his tongue. "I'm going to put my hand between your legs. Say yes."

"Yes." Her agreement came with ease. "You must think I'm a wanton woman."

"No, you're simply allowing your passionate nature its release." He nudged her legs apart, slid one hand underneath the long folds of her chemise and cupped her mound. "Now I'm going to touch inside of you."

"Can I touch you too?"

"Maybe later." With a wicked grin, he covered her mouth and kissed her with such sweet abandon. She wrapped her arms around his neck, speared her fingers into his silky hair and held on as he moved his fingers back and forth along her lower folds. Gazing into her eyes, he pushed one finger deep inside her then rattled off a long stream of Italian.

"Oh my." Aroused beyond measure, she arched her

124

back and he licked across both her nipples, the lazy stroke of his tongue sending a bolt of pure pleasure rushing through her core and dampening her inner thighs. He devoured her breasts, a second finger pushing in, then he caressed a spot that had her crying out. Too much. She flew, bright lights suddenly flaring behind her closed eyes and taking her away to another realm she'd never visited before.

Slowly, she came back down and when she opened her eyes, he knelt over her on the bed, the front flap of his breeches loose and his shaft in hand. He stroked his cock in a show of sensual beauty she'd never thought to behold. He worked himself and with a deep and agonizing moan, the head of his cock turning a deep shade of purple, he thrust his cock into her chemise covered hip, shuddered and splashed his seed across the covers.

She closed her eyes again as he sank down on top of her, his heavenly weight there one moment then suddenly gone the next.

Thwack.

A hooded man swung a baton.

Anteros tussled and fought and she screamed.

A jagged scar slashed the intruder's cheek. Bruno.

Hauling her chemise up, she struggled to her feet then got knocked to the floor as the two men brawled. Bruno slammed his head into Anteros's middle and Anteros went sailing, cracked his head on one of the bedposts and slumped to the ground.

A vein throbbed in Bruno's forehead as he snarled at her.

He swung his fist and everything went dark.

Chapter 11

Disorientated and groggy, Anteros lifted his thumping head from the floor of his bedchamber.

He pushed to his feet, his room spinning.

Darkness outside his window. Darkness inside.

Only a few embers still glowed in his hearth.

Rubbing the back of his head, he winced at the large lump and—Olivia. He'd brought Olivia home with him from Hyde Park. He jerked the waistband of his breeches up, fastened the front flap and almost tripped on a baton. A lump of royal-blue fabric lay rumpled on the floor at his feet, a patch of cream silk with it. A blouse. A petite pair of riding boots were placed before the hearth to dry, lady's stockings discarded to one side.

His trunk.

His weapons sat propped against the side of it.

Nothing else.

The change of clothes he'd collected from Adrestia's wardrobe were gone.

He roared, his bellow ricocheting off the walls and echoing in his ears.

Footsteps pounded.

Bellini scuttled inside, his ever-efficient butler glancing wildly about. "Is everything all right, sir?"

"Find Giovani and my sister. Ensure no harm has come to Adrestia."

"What's happened?" Giovani appeared in the doorway. "I heard your yell."

"What time is it?"

"Six. Adrestia and I have not long returned from the park."

"Bruno is what's happened and when I find him, I'll wring his blasted neck and make sure he dies with the utmost pain I can inflict." Stumbling to his dresser, he tried to keep his focus as everything continued to sway. "Help me find my woman."

"Lady Olivia is here?" Giovani frowned as he searched the room.

"She was. I brought her home with me following our sail along the Serpentine. She got drenched and with my residence being far closer than hers, I wished to see her changed into dry clothing. I placed one of Adrestia's gowns on my trunk for her to change into and it's gone. Bruno took her. We need to find her, now." He dragged on a white tunic with billowy sleeves.

"Anteros?" Adrestia flew into his bedchamber in her forest-green riding habit, her dark locks flying. "What's going on?"

"Bruno attacked me, then took Olivia with him. We need to find them both."

"Why would Bruno have taken Olivia?" His sister stepped on something that crunched under her feet. She stepped back, scooped a piece of paper from the floor, his name emblazoned across the front.

"Give it to me." She did and he unfolded the note and read the words for both his sister and Giovani to hear.

"Your Royal Highness,

I act under direct orders from your father to retrieve Lady Olivia Trentbury and to bring her directly to him. We will be awaiting your arrival at Paradiso, although don't expect the lady to remain alive for long. Her death is assured, while your marriage to another is now certain. I'm sure you can guess as to whom.

Bruno."

Fury raged inside him as never before. "Not only will I kill Bruno, but I'll kill Father as well if he lays a hand on Olivia."

"We need a plan of attack." Adrestia clutched one hand to her middle. "Bruno is an imbecile for stealing Olivia away from you. We'll catch up to him before he reaches Paradiso. Goodness, I can't believe Father would have asked Bruno to do such a thing."

"Father must have planned all of this." He strapped on his sword belt and daggers, although he never would have thought Father would go this far either. Unfortunately, he shouldn't have underestimated his sire. "I need to inform Lady Winterly of her daughter's kidnapping. I'll write her a letter and have it dispatched immediately. We set sail this eve, on the high tide."

"I'll ready the crew." Giovani stormed out, calling over his shoulder, "I'll meet you both at the docks."

Facing his sister, his heartbeat a raging mess, he muttered, "Shira never warned me that Olivia would be stolen from me, although she did proclaim that my angel would be both the intervention and the prevention of my death, that I'm to keep her at my side, at all times, day and night, whether I am on English soil or sailing the dangerous waters I know so well. I have failed her thus far. I won't fail her again."

"I'll sail The Decadence alongside The Cobra."

"Let's pack and be away." He charged down the passageway to his study, his sister racing to her bedchamber. Bellini followed him inside his sanctuary and stood with his hands clasped behind his back. While his butler awaited his orders, he settled himself at his chunky oak desk, his leather chair creaking and the fire crackling in the hearth. He shoved a pile of papers to one side.

"If I'd known—"

He raised a hand and cut Bellini off. "I'm the one who should have known Bruno might strike out against me." He'd never hold his butler responsible for Bruno's dastardly actions. "Bruno is dishonorable, devious, and immoral. He not only raised a hand against me, but he has now kidnapped an innocent lady. You can be assured when I find him, I will end his life."

"I find it almost unbelievable he struck his own prince." Bellini's brows drew together, his scowl fierce, his butler well aware of his parentage since the man was a trusted member of his staff. "I heard you say you're sailing on the high tide, sir."

"Yes, I'll be leaving as soon as I've written a letter to Lady Olivia's mother, the dowager Countess of Winterly, a letter which I need you to deliver directly to her at the Earl of Winterly's townhouse. In the meantime, I need you to ready all I'll require for my trip to Paradiso."

"I'll pack your belongings right away." His butler whisked out the door.

It appeared Father had never intended for him to marry Olivia. And here he'd thought he was the one instigating a ruse. Obviously, he'd been playing right into Father's hands all along. His sire now held his woman as leverage and he'd soon be forced to speak vows with the Archduchess Clementina. He'd do so too. To ensure Olivia's survival.

He drew forth a leaf of paper, and with his fear for Olivia growing stronger as each second ticked by, he dipped his quill into the inkwell and wrote.

Dear Lady Winterly,

I must beg your forgiveness, madam, for this letter I write is of a distressing nature. A man in my father's employ has taken your daughter as his hostage this day and set sail for the island of Paradiso off the coastline of Sicily. I must set sail after him, immediately, so I can claim her back. I give you my word I shall retrieve Olivia and return her safely home to you.

Yours with unfailing loyalty,
Anteros Bourbon.

After folding the letter, he poured wax and sealed it with his cobra ring. Scraping a hand across his unshaven jaw, he crossed to his side table and gulped brandy directly from the decanter. Out his study window, the night sky remained dark and black, rain sleeting down and pinging off the glass. Guilt rose sharp and hard in his chest. Olivia had never asked for this when she'd offered him her aid. Now he'd placed her life in danger.

Hell, he was such an idiot for not considering how far Father would go in ensuring he got his way.

He threw the empty decanter into the fire and it smashed into a million glittering shards. His heart was no better off, just as completely broken as the fine crystal he'd tossed.

Chapter 12

Hot. So hot. Olivia opened her heavy eyelids and sweat dribbled into her eyes and hazed her vision. She blinked repeatedly then squinted as a sliver of light shone on the strangest angle from somewhere above her head.

Lying on her side wrapped in a blanket, she tried to move her arms and legs, but only managed to tighten corded linen bound around her ankles and wrists, both roped together behind her back and making her arch awkwardly. Her back and shoulders throbbed. Her head thumped as if horses stampeded within.

She tried to breathe through the chaos storming through her head.

Wooden boards all around her. She must be in a crate, and that light streaming from between two planks, possibly the lid.

Clothes had been stuffed in beside her, the red velvet gown and black hooded cloak.

Pushing with her tongue, she tried to spit out a foul-tasting gag stuffed in her mouth, except another piece of linen held it firmly in place around her head. Everything dipped and rolled and she dry heaved. She had to get out of here, wherever here was.

More rolling, and she slid across a floor, the crate banging into something. Rolling back. Another thump. She must be on board a vessel.

A whiff of sea salt drifted through the cracks.

Yes, definitely a vessel.

Tears streaked down her cheeks and puddled on the scratchy wooden crating underneath her. Bruno had attacked Anteros. She should have fought Bruno too. Oh, and Mama. She would be beside herself with fear when she learnt of what had happened. "I need you, Anteros," she mumbled into the cloth. "Find me. Rescue me. Please come."

Gritting her teeth, she pushed her cheek against the side of the crate and scraped the binding from her mouth. Success. She pushed the gag free and screamed.

JOANNE WADSWORTH

Chapter 13

"Is the coach ready?" In the downstairs foyer, Anteros pushed his arms into the sleeves of his black greatcoat which Bellini held out for him.

"Yes. All is packed, and I shall deliver your letter directly to the dowager countess." His butler clipped his heels together. "Safe travels to Paradiso, sir."

"I'm ready as well." Adrestia swept down the stairwell in beige breeches and knee-high boots, her midnight black hair pulled back with a strip of leather at her nape, a thick burgundy woolen coat flapping about her ankles.

"Giovani sent word that all provisions have been loaded." He opened the door for her and she strode through.

"Yes, I heard." Slotting a curved dagger in the leather sheath at her hip, she appeared every inch his sister, the formidable *sorella del cobra.*

"It's time to catch and kill the spy." He settled himself inside his coach on the plush golden velvet squabs, his driver bounding into his seat atop the conveyance. They

134

jerked forward and bumped along the streets toward the docks. Itching to be at the helm of his ship and underway, he grasped his knees, his knuckles going white.

"We'll find her before we reach Paradiso." Adrestia rested her leather gloved hand over his.

"Bruno's attack was completely orchestrated. He came straight at me with a baton." He didn't doubt Bruno had already booked passage on a merchant ship too, which was why he'd taken the risk of entering his bedchamber to make a grab for Olivia. He had to have been running out of time. "There are thousands of ships moored along the length of the River Thames. It's the largest, busiest port in the world, with hundreds of those ships carrying passengers bound for the Mediterranean." The window curtain swayed, the brick warehouses lining the docks outside passing by in a blur. "He knows we'll struggle to catch up to him, particularly when we have to stop every single vessel en route to Sicily to see if it's carrying Olivia."

"We'll target every merchant ship we can." An unflappable answer from his sister, a squeeze of his hand too as he continued to stare out the window. "Look at me, Anteros." A gentle request.

"*Sì?*" He struggled to return his gaze to hers, but torturously, he did.

"Do you love her?" Adrestia cupped his cheek.

"I'd be a fool to fall in love with any woman. Father desires her death, and I fear ever telling her the truth about who I truly am—a lost Prince of Naples and Sicily. After I rescue her, it will be best if I remain out of her life."

"She won't like that."

"She won't have any choice." The carriage slowed,

rounded the corner to where his ships bobbed at berth. Once they rocked to a halt, he stepped down onto the wooden platform, offered his sister a hand and pulled her into a fierce hug. In her ear, he murmured, "I love you. Sail directly alongside me. Do you hear?"

"I'll be right beside you. I love you too." She squeezed him back, broke away and marched up the gangplank to her ship. His sister took her position at the helm of her vessel, calling orders to her crew as she did.

The moon broke through a heavy patch of black cloud and reflected its watery-white glow off the rippling waters of the Thames. With the wind blowing his greatcoat against his legs, he stormed onto his ship. His crew swarmed the rain slick deck as they stacked crates and carried supplies for the journey below into the hold.

He climbed the short flight of stairs to the upper deck and rested his hands on the smooth, rounded lines of the wheel. Corded grooves in the solid wood warmed his palms and strength infused him. He would find Olivia. He'd allow no other outcome.

"Cap'n!" A shout from Wills as he sprinted down the walkway to where his men now loaded the last crate on board. The boy jumped, landed on the boarding plank and raced in a blur past Giovani toward him. Skidding to a halt next to the wheel, the lad half bent over and gasped for breath.

"What's happened?" He lowered himself to Wills' height and squeezed his shoulder. The lad's hands shook on his knees. "Take deep breaths."

"Wills?" Giovani joined them, hunkered down too. "What's wrong, lad?"

The boy straightened, his brown woolen jacket smeared with dirt, his cheeks too. He swiped his sleeve across his face and eyed Anteros, clear worry clouding his eyes. "I was downstairs when Bruno slunk into your house. He's been followin' ye everywhere and I saw him leave too. He had something bundled in his arms, wrapped in a blanket. I thought he'd killed someone. It looked like a body ye see, in the blanket. I hid when Bruno ducked outside. He hailed a hackney and I jumped onto the backboard and kept my head down. We traveled all the way to the eastern embarkin' quay where he boarded *The Venture*, a merchant ship sailin' for Sicily then Greece."

He hauled Wills into his arms and hugged the lad, never more grateful. "You've done extremely well, Wills. Bruno kidnapped Lady Olivia a few hours ago and intends on sailing to Paradiso. This information you've now brought us will save us a great deal of time. Now I know exactly which ship she's on." He jerked his chin toward the companionway leading below deck. "Find a bunk. You're coming with me on this trip."

"Aye, aye, Cap'n." Wills saluted him.

He rose and stalked to the edge of the upper deck and gripped the railing. Across from him, Adrestia perused maps at her helm as she marked her course. Leaning out, he called, "Wills spotted Bruno leaving the house with Olivia. He followed him to the eastern embarking quay. We're searching for The Venture."

Eyes wide, she stared at him, then she beamed. "We'll find her."

"Upon my soul, we will."

"Release the ropes!" Adrestia bellowed to her crew.

"It's time to depart."

"All to stations," he ordered his own men. "Unfurl the sails."

Three of his crew pushed them off the wharf, bounded back on board and coiled the ropes. Men scurried up the rigging and dropped the sails. The wind hit them with a hearty *thwap*, and he steered them from their berth through the dark of the night along the muddied, churning waters toward the English Channel.

Chapter 14

Olivia tried to shove against whatever held her down.

"Stay still, my lady." A feminine voice. "You're free of that awful crate and now lying safe in a bed. This is your cabin for the duration of your trip to Sicily. You're on board The Venture."

"Bed?" She forced her eyes open then blinked at the harsh brightness of sunshine streaming through a square section of windows gone blurry with salty sea spray. Everything spun then slowly settled a little.

"Yes, a bed." The feminine voice belonged to a young woman wearing a high-collared navy gown buttoned to her chin. Glossy brown curls, her brown eyes filled with clear worry. The lady slowly released her wrists and straightened. "How do you feel?"

"Dizzy, light-headed, achy." Overhead, a gauzy yellow-colored canopy shifted over her head, moving with the gentle rock under the bed. Paneled walls were painted white, while high wooden beams crossed the ceiling. Two glass lamps swayed from the two central ceiling beams. In one corner sat a bench seat holding dark yellow squabs. A ship. She was definitely on board a ship. She pressed a hand to her dry and sore throat. "Is there water, or something I can drink?"

"Your husband, Signore Bruno, asked a maid to leave a tray for you, which included a pot of tea. I'll pour you a cup." The petite woman swished to a side table next to a washbasin. Steam curled from the spout of a teapot.

She rubbed her reddened wrists, her knuckles scraped red and raw. Taking care, she pushed upright and pressed her back against the headboard. A white bedsheet covered her from the waist down, a clean shift now donned in place of the chemise she'd last been wearing, and her right cheek, oh, it ached and when she touched it, her fingers came away with an icky green paste on them.

"You had a nasty scrape on your cheek. Try not to touch it until it's all healed. I applied plantain herb." The woman poured tea into a cup, added a splash of milk and a spoonful of honey then sat on the bed beside her before carefully turning the cup on the saucer so she could take it from her. "My grandmother had an herb garden. As a child I learnt at her knee all about the healing qualities of various herbs. Plantain is used for cleansing wounds and preventing infection."

"Thank you for tending to my injuries." She accepted the offered cup and sipped. Warmth streaked to her belly, the honey deliciously sweet and the drink soothing her parched throat. "Might I ask who you are?"

"Miss Violet Russo, from Dartford."

"London?"

"Yes, although I'm now traveling to Sicily. My father recently passed away and left me a rather large inheritance, which included a palazzo in Palermo. He was Sicilian, my mother English."

"I'm so sorry for your loss, Miss Russo."

"Violet, and I barely knew him. My mother's parents raised me after my mother passed away, twenty-five years ago now. My father only ever visited me a handful of times in Dartford over the years." A wave of her hand. "A long time ago now. I've always wanted to travel, particularly to Sicily, my father's homeland. Now I am."

"Alone?"

"I'm thirty, a rather decrepit age. I've chosen to embrace my spinsterhood. I'll employ a maid and housekeeper once I arrive at my new home." She shuffled closer and patted her hand. "Now, tell me who you are, because I didn't believe for one moment that Signore Bruno was actually your husband. He decreed that your marriage was a clandestine one, that he had to spirit you safely away from England, but, well I saw that crate." Violet frowned something fierce. "Atrocious, I tell you. When I heard your screams from the cabin next to mine, I rushed over and found Signore Bruno being rough with you, and all while you were still bound and restrained inside your crated prison."

"I'm Lady Olivia Trentbury. Bruno kidnapped me. We aren't husband and wife, not at all."

"Which is as I thought when he hauled you from the crate and dumped you on his bed, all without showing even an ounce of care for you. May I call you Olivia?"

"Yes, please do." She searched Violet's gaze. "The

last thing I remember was being in the crate and screaming for help."

"I demanded Bruno remove your bindings and bring you directly to my cabin so I could tend to your wounds, which thankfully he did, although that's when he left us both and locked my cabin door behind him. I thumped the door and called out until an officer finally came. Unfortunately, the officer couldn't help me. I demanded to see the captain, who then arrived along with Bruno. Your kidnapper has convinced the captain of this ship that you're his wife and I'm his sister, that the two of us are unruly ladies and not to be believed should we speak out against him. Thus, we remain locked inside my cabin."

"Bruno's cabin is next to yours, correct?" Her head was still a little foggy.

"Yes, down the companionway, on the port side, a cabin which is booked for himself and you, his wife." Violet blew out a long breath, her shoulders slumping. "I've let you down by not being able to secure our freedom. I'm so sorry. Since I boarded on my own, and no one on this ship can confirm I'm speaking the truth, it's his word against mine."

"I'll speak to the captain too." She rubbed Violet's shoulder. "None of this is your fault."

"You can try speaking to him, but Bruno carries a letter from the King of Sicily—Ferdinand III of the House of Bourbon. It states Bruno's position amongst the king's staff and that he must be shown every courtesy on his return to Sicily. The captain handed me the letter and it indeed holds the king's signature and seal. I don't see a way out of this mess."

"Wait." She jerked, spilling her tea onto the saucer. "Bruno is in the possession of a letter from King Ferdinand?"

"Yes, that's exactly what I said." Violet nudged her to drink. "Your head will be a little cloudy until you regain your strength. Your voice is rather raspy too. The honey I added to your tea will help soothe it."

Shocked, her mind spun in a hundred different directions. She sipped the soothing tea and tried to make sense of everything.

Wringing her hands, Violet rose and paced the cabin. "We need to ascertain the truth of all that's happened. If you're willing to shed some light on what you know, we might be able to uncover what's going on and find an answer."

"Of course I'll share whatever I know." She'd now unwittingly involved an innocent lady in her abduction, a lovely and caring young woman. "I've not known Bruno long."

"How did you first meet him?" A quick return to her bedside, Violet's navy skirts swishing.

"Bruno was placed on board Captain Anteros Bourbon's ship by the captain's father. When Captain Bourbon returned to England only a few days ago, Bruno was tailing him. That's when I met Bruno, through the captain."

"Is Captain Bourbon aligned in anyway with House of Bourbon? The last name of Bourbon is the same, which is impossible to miss."

"Bourbon is a common family surname." She'd never associated Anteros's surname with the Royal House of

Bourbon.

"It is common, but still a link we can't dismiss in relation to our current situation." Violet rolled a hand. "Please continue."

"Good grief. You're right. It is a link we can't dismiss." Which would then point to Ferdinand being Captain Bourbon's father. Oh my word. That would explain how Anteros had so easily gained an invitation to the Duchess of Genoa's ball being held at the Royal Palace of Palermo. She gulped another mouthful of tea.

Violet arched a brow. "You appear to be thinking rather deeply. Do share."

"Bruno kidnapped me because I'm marrying another man, or supposedly I am."

"Supposedly?" Eyes flaring wide, Violet leaned in. "I would never betray your confidence should you choose to place your trust in me."

"Since we're both now locked in here together, and you've been ever so helpful and truthful, I shall be completely truthful in return. Although whatever I say mustn't go any further than the two of us. Swear it won't."

"I swear." Violet crossed her heart.

"I'm in love with a rather secretive man—Captain Bourbon. A few days ago he came to me needing my aid in an elaborate ruse. That is how we're 'supposedly' getting married. It's all a ploy in order to waylay his father who has demanded Anteros wed a lady he's chosen for him. So, if Anteros is King Ferdinand's son, not that Anteros has actually told me that, but if the king is his father, then a kidnapping makes sense. Ferdinand wouldn't want me upsetting his grand plans for his son, not when the lady he's chosen for him is the Archduchess Clementina of Austria."

"Oh, such intrigue." Violet gasped into her palm.

A jangle of keys and the door swung open.

Bruno snarled as he ducked his head under the low entranceway.

Her abductor had returned.

Chapter 15

Once clear of England's shores, Anteros took the swiftest sea route along the coastline of Portugal toward the jutting southern point of Spain's Gibraltar. Over the long hours and even longer days that passed, he barely left his position at the wheel. Here, he could keep a closer eye on the waters along the common trade route toward Sicily.

Lifting his telescope to his eye for the hundredth time that day, he once again searched for any sign of the ship he chased. Abreast of him where she had clean wind, Adrestia too held her scope to her eye, their two ships slicing through the waves side by side.

Under a warm blue sky with only a streak of white cloud hazing the horizon, his sister brought her ship closer then handed the wheel to her first mate. In soft rawhide breeches and a white tunic, clothing she always wore while captaining her ship, his sister gripped the rail on the upper deck and called, "How are you?"

"Angry. Determined. Frustrated." Tension thrummed

through him as he scrubbed a hand across the back of his neck and tried to ease some of the stiffness and the strain the past ten days of being without Olivia had caused him. His head hurt with how much he'd been thinking about her, while his heart had become an aching, endless, screaming pit of pain. His need to see her, to hold her, to keep her safe in his embrace was a fierce desire that couldn't be contained.

Do you love her? His sister's words from that fateful night when Bruno had kidnapped Olivia filled his head.

I'd be a fool to fall in love with any woman.

A damned fool. Not only did danger lurk for those closest to him, but he feared ever telling her the truth about who he truly was.

"I need to keep a lookout," he called to Adrestia and with his scope back at his eye, he narrowed his gaze and— was that a sail in the distance? He turned the wheel a touch and adjusted his course, Adrestia doing the same, his sister clearly spotting the same sail.

Gritting his teeth, he waited and waited as long hours passed, until finally he'd made enough ground on the ship to uncover more through his scope. A flag flew from the top of the ship's mizzenmast—the British flag. The Venture was a British ship. A few passengers strolled the deck, ladies with parasols raised and gentlemen offering their arms, hats atop their heads. The crew worked the rigging. Definitely a commuter ship. He focused his scope on the solid paneling of the ship's stern, right between the high curved scrollwork cresting the top and the long run of square-cut windows in the center. In an elegant script blazed the ship's name—*The Venture.*

Fierce emotions roared through him. Olivia was so close.

He lowered his scope, his entire body shuddering with need, the venomous hiss of the cobra deep within him lifting its head as he prepared to strike.

Chapter 16

Grasping the yellow skirts of the gown she'd borrowed from Violet's traveling trunk at the end of the bed they'd both slept in these past ten days, Olivia paced the confines of their prison. Overhead, the golden glow of the candlelit lamps swayed light into the darkened corners, the hour now close to midnight. Day eleven was about to begin. Violet sat on the corner bench seat under the cabin window with her embroidery in hand and a reel of vibrant turquoise cotton rolling back and forth across the dark yellow squabs, the rocking of the ship as endless as their tortuous time at sea had been.

When they'd sailed past Gibraltar a few days ago and crossed into the Mediterranean, land had been visible out their port window for a short time. Now, only the endless night-shrouded blue of the sea with its white-tipped waves washed in a silvery hue under the moonlight, spread for as far as the eye could see.

"Why don't you come and embroider with me? Your

angel tapestry is taking wonderful form. I'm looking forward to seeing it all complete. I'm sure your mama will love it." Violet held out the embroidery kit which she'd been working on during the long days of their confinement. She'd wanted to recreate a piece of her time with Anteros, so she'd stitched the angel sculpture from Grace Hall and the garden bed surrounding it. She'd told Violet all about her family, Mama and her brothers and sisters, while Violet had shared stories about her late mother and grandparents in return.

She eased onto the bench seat next to her friend, rested a hand on Violet's hand as she stitched. "I'm not sure what I would have done without you these past ten days."

"You haven't exactly had a choice but to accept my company." A teasing twinkle lit Violet's eyes, her way of lightening the mood. "How does your cheek feel?"

"It's healed, and my bruises are beginning to fade." She'd been covered in them, a motley number spread in various places. Bruno had certainly hurt her while she'd been out of it, but at least she'd retained very little memory of that time, other than for the odd flash of recall in between the time she'd been taken and then meeting Violet. "Once we reach land, which can't be far away, we must do whatever we can to escape Bruno."

"We will both kick and scream until we can get away from him." A firm nod from Violet. "Then we flee to my late father's palazzo, my palazzo now. I have the address, and coin tucked away in my pocket."

They'd both agreed they must be ready to run with only the clothing they had on them, which meant sleeping fully clothed at night, slippers on their feet too.

A knock rattled the door then the scrape of the key turned in the lock. Bruno ducked his head under the low doorframe as he entered. Twice a day, he allowed the young Portuguese maid on board—who unfortunately spoke not a word of English—to bring them their morning and evening meals. Never did he remain with them for long though, other than to gloat and smirk at his ingeniousness. Since he'd visited twice already today, this third visit was most unusual.

She rose to her feet, her hands fisted at her sides. "Why are you gracing us with your despicable presence once again this day?"

"It appears your dour mood never lifts." His gaze dropped to the low neckline of her gown, a greediness flickering in his beady black eyes which made her skin crawl.

"If you touch me again…" He'd tried the second day they'd been out at sea, but Violet had tossed the basin of water on him, then picked up a chair to swing next. Bruno had backed away, but not without sending her a perverted look which made her itch with revulsion.

"We have two more days at sea, possibly less if the winds continue to remain favorable. Palermo first, then we'll hire a sailboat to cross the short distance to Paradiso." He leaned against the closed door, removed a flask hooked to his belt, uncorked it and swigged a mouthful of whatever foul brew he kept in it.

"How long have you served your liege?" Whenever she could, she tried to glean more information about King Ferdinand from him, not that Bruno was very forthcoming with information. All she'd gotten so far was uncommitted grunts here and there. Even when she'd asked outright if Anteros was in fact the king's son, he'd not answered her. That didn't matter. She and Violet both firmly believed Anteros was after they'd pieced together all the information. Anteros had clearly kept his identity a secret, for years and years, those around him keeping it too.

"I know your opinion of me." Bruno held her gaze. "You believe I have a rotten black soul for having torn you away from your loved ones."

"No, I don't believe you have a soul at all."

"Anteros will soon be speaking vows with another lady." He curled one corner of his lips up. "You'd best accept that."

"The other lady is but a girl of sixteen," Violet stated as she made a move from the squabs.

"You two are in league, I see." He glared from Violet to her.

She raised a hand to halt her friend from venturing any closer to Bruno. Ensuring she continued the ruse Anteros had asked of her was all-important, so she added, "Anteros never breaks his word. He and I will soon speak vows and I will be his wife. He holds no affection for the archduchess."

"Captain Bourbon will submit to his father's will, otherwise he'll be forcing you to suffer the consequences of his actions. Above all else, the captain is a man who protects the innocent. I left him a letter before carting you away, ensuring he knew your life was at stake."

"You are an insufferable beast."

"When we reach Paradiso, I intend on teaching you a better way of using your swift tongue." He gripped his crotch and gave it a yank.

"Get out of here." She jabbed a finger at the door.

Boom!

The door shattered into pieces, the vessel tilting sharply.

She got thrown and hit the floor, Bruno slamming down on top of her.

"Go Violet. Get out of here," she wheezed from underneath Bruno's heavy weight.

"No, I'm not leaving without you." Violet stumbled across, yanked at Bruno's legs and tried to drag him off her. "Help me push."

The ship listed further. Passengers screamed from the companionway. A hole now lay where the door had been. Olivia heaved and Bruno rolled off and thumped onto the floor. Blood oozed from a spear of wood sticking out of his side. He moaned, and she scrambled clear, grasped Violet's hand and staggered into the smoking mess along the passageway.

Bruno's bellow echoed from behind them.

An officer herded them and other passengers toward the stairs. "We're under attack from corsairs. Everyone to starboard. Passengers will be loaded onto the boats."

She and Violet rushed upstairs, jostling to get there faster. They coughed and spluttered as they reached the deck. Acrid smoke clouded everywhere. Rubble littered the foredeck. Sailors scurried about as they fed the cannons. The captain bellowed orders from the helm. Sheer mayhem ensued as she held tight to Violet's hand.

"Incoming," one of the crew yelled from the crows' nest.

"Get down." The officer close behind them pushed her and Violet to the deck and covered them.

A ball hit near the mizzenmast and blasted boards everywhere, a hole opening up in the deck to the floor below.

A seventy-gun warship slammed into their side and corsairs wearing strips of leather knotted through their hair tossed grappling hooks onto the masts and swung on board with a thunderous battle cry. Leery grins, blackened teeth, curved swords, thick beards, dirks flying.

The officer heaved to his feet, brandished his saber and launched at the corsair bearing down on them. The pirate ducked low and swung hard at the officer. Blood splattered, their protector hitting the ground with a sickening thud, his gut sliced open.

This couldn't be happening.

This had to be a nightmare.

Surely she'd awaken any moment and—

The corsair's dark shadow fell over her and Violet, his leather vest shredded at the hem, a gold tooth gleaming and spittle flying from his mouth. "You two will fetch a pretty penny at the souk in Algiers."

Another officer bounded toward them with his saber raised and the pirate heaved his curved blade high. The two men fought, steel clanging loud against steel. A fire blazed, a mast crashing to the deck and the crows' nest toppling with a shuddering *crash*. More shouts.

The battle filled the air. So too did screams from the passengers. Many jumped over the side. She clutched Violet closer, hugging her, her friend's face streaked with soot. "We have to get off this ship. Can you swim, Violet?"

The ship tilted farther and seawater gushed in.

"Yes, but not in this gown," Violet yelled over the howling wind and the violence of the battle.

"Then we strip to our undergarments." She tore at the front fastenings of her gown, while Violet did the same, seawater now up to their knees.

In naught but her shift, she scrambled onto the top rail of the sinking ship, seized Violet's hand and jumped over the side. They hit the icy water with a scream, then went down, down and down. Turbulent waters surged all around. Kicking, they both pushed back to the surface. Crashing waves tossed them about, shoving them farther from the burning vessel.

A cry from Violet as she jabbed a finger to the west. "Look, two more vessels approach."

Two ninety-gun warships cut through the moonlit dark, both firing upon the corsairs' seventy-gun frigate. From the mizzenmasts of both vessels flew flags with a hissing snake. "Anteros and Adrestia are here," she screamed to Violet.

"Oh my word." Violet's face went pale under the streaky soot.

Armed men from both Anteros and Adrestia's warships swung across to the sinking ship, Giovani and Anteros leading the raid.

"Anteros!" She yelled his name, but her cry got lost in the whistling wind rushing all about.

On the foredeck, Anteros and Giovani fought side by side, both clashing with the corsairs intent on attacking and raiding.

Another fierce battle cry. Bruno charged through the

smoke and chaos, one hand clutching his bleeding side and the other his saber. Anteros met him head-on, swung and caught Bruno's blade dead center. A blur of movement, the two of them battling hard. Anteros lunged and parried, blocking each of Bruno's strikes, then one jarring hit from Bruno had Anteros falling back. He splashed into the water on deck, shoved to his feet and bounded forward.

Anteros ducked another of Bruno's blows then slammed into Bruno and shoved him toward the blazing inferno. Bruno went down with a roar. Anteros stared down at him, said something, then swung. Bruno's head flew from his shoulders and she gagged. Such a violent death.

Anteros bellowed her name, his shouts echoing across the waves as he searched the deck for her. Again she yelled, and this time he jerked a look toward her and—

He sheathed his blade and dove over the rail, Giovani diving right into the swell after him. The water swallowed both men whole, then her captain emerged and cut through the waves. He swam and grabbed her around the waist, worry and fear slashing his face. "Are you all right?"

"I can't believe you're here." She stared into his piercing sapphire eyes. "How did you—"

"I've been searching for you since Bruno stole you away." He firmed his hold on her, the current twisting and turning them all around.

She gulped in great drafts of air. "Please, tell me I'm not dreaming. You are a sight to behold."

"You're not dreaming, *Amore*. I'm so sorry. I should have gotten to you far sooner." He cupped the back of her head and drew her closer against him, his dark hair floating around his neck as he treaded water for them both.

"You truly are real." His body was solid, his flesh warm, and his hold gloriously tight. She snatched his shirtfront as over his shoulder, the ship she'd been held hostage on for the past week and a half sank below the water, a wave washing out and the corsairs who'd attacked now swimming back to their pirate ship.

"Let's get these ladies on board," Anteros commanded Giovani who had clasped Violet's waist and currently aided her in staying afloat.

Giovani held Violet tight as he kicked them both toward Anteros's ship, Anteros keeping one firm arm around her waist as he cut a fast path directly behind the others.

They made the ship and Giovani and Violet got hauled on board. Cheers erupted from Anteros's men, while Adrestia sobbed as she tried to reach over the side for her. "Reach for my hand, Olivia."

"You're next." Anteros boosted her upward and Adrestia and Giovani both caught her hands and tugged her on board. She got swamped in Adrestia's hold, her friend squeezing the life out of her, Wills suddenly appearing in between them and hugging her too. She hugged Wills back, tears blurring her own eyes. Anteros climbed the rope and swung over the railing behind her, his booted feet thumping on the deck. He pulled her from Wills and Adrestia, swept her hair back from her brow and touched a spot that throbbed. "There's a small gash. Are you hurt anywhere else?"

"No, I don't think so." In her drenched shift which clung to her, she clutched Violet's hand and dragged her friend back to her side. "Let me introduce you all to Miss

Violet Russo. She and I have become rather close during our joint imprisonment at Bruno's hands. She got caught up in the whole mess. Violet, this is Captain Anteros Bourbon, Giovani, and Miss Adrestia Bourbon."

"It's a pleasure to meet you Miss Russo." Anteros dipped his head.

"Well, it's a delight to finally meet you, Captain Bourbon. An absolute delight." Violet wrapped her arms around herself as she shivered. "You have excellent timing by the way. Olivia and I were just in need of your rescue. It was good of you to arrive when you did."

"My apologies for not arriving sooner. You're cold. Let me see to that." Anteros grasped Wills' shoulder. "Show Miss Russo to a cabin. Ensure she has all she needs, warm clothes and food, do you understand?"

"Aye, Cap'n."

"I'll see you soon." Violet squeezed her hand then disappeared with Wills below deck.

More passengers got pulled onto The Cobra and The Decadence, all who'd need care this night. Anteros slapped Giovani on the back. "Fish everyone from the sea, raise the sails and set course for Paradiso. Also make certain the corsairs don't follow us. I need to go and look after my angel."

"Aye, Captain." Giovani jogged up the stairs to the wheel.

"We will speak after Anteros has seen to your needs." Adrestia kissed her cheek then swung back on board The Decadence, orders flying to her crew to aid the survivors on board.

"You certainly do have excellent timing." She cupped

Anteros's cheeks in her hands, uncaring of who saw her or the rip in her shift, the hem dragging on the deck. She rubbed her thumbs under the dark circles shadowing his eyes. "Take me to your cabin, Captain."

"If that's an order, then I'm at your command." He scooped her into his arms and carried her across the deck, jogged down the stairs and walked along the companionway.

"I feared never seeing you again." She snuggled her head against his shoulder as he stepped into a well-appointed cabin with black lacquered cabinets lining two of the four walls, a monstrous bed pressed against one wall and a chunky oak desk in the far corner. Papers and rolled maps were heaped on top of the desk, an elegant settee and armchair forming a sitting area in front of it, this cabin far larger than any she'd ever seen before. Oil burned in an iron wall sconce and cast a gentle glow about his private quarters.

"I feared the same with you." He closed the door with one foot and seated her onto the end of his bed covered in a thick sapphire-colored quilt. Kneeling at her feet, his fingers digging into her sides, he rested his forehead against her forehead, their noses touching.

"You killed Bruno, and I'm exceedingly grateful you did, not that a lady should say such a thing after I watched his beheading, but he was a wretched soul, dark to his very depths."

"I wish I could raise him from the dead just so I can kill him again." A lift of his gaze back to hers. "He didn't suffer nearly enough for my liking. How did you come to meet Violet?"

"Violet saved me from Bruno. If it weren't for her I would still be stuck in a crate in Bruno's cabin, no doubt bound and gagged. Instead, Violet and I have spent the entire trip confined to her cabin, unable to seek help from an officer or even the captain. Bruno—"

"Don't say his name again, not right now." He pressed a finger to her lips. "I'm going to undress you. I need to ascertain for myself if you're in good health. Being dumped in the sea can cause your skin to become numb to the cold and therefore injuries can go unnoticed."

"I don't hurt anywhere, not now I'm back with you." She touched the spot on her forehead where he'd noted a gash, but no blood came away on her fingers. "This scrape will likely heal on its own."

"I believe so too."

"My body does feel numb from the cold though." She wriggled forward and kissed his chin. She had no intention of holding back in showing her affection for him, not when tonight could have ended very differently. Losing him. Never knowing his touch. Those were things she never wanted to imagine again. "I need you, Anteros. I want to feel your mouth on mine, your hands roaming my body, your heat caressing my skin. I want to feel alive again, for you to take this awful numbness away. Will you make love to me?"

"You are painfully beautiful, and I am already decidedly drunk on the returned sight of you." He pushed to his feet, his wet tunic plastered to his chest, the white cotton molding his muscled arms and rippling abs. Water dripped from his tight-fitting black breeches, his strong legs planted wide and his feet squelching in his boots. He searched her gaze. "Are you certain?"

"Exceedingly certain."

"*Il mio bellissimo angelo,* I want to feel alive again too." He tugged her to her feet, then suddenly lowered to a crouch.

"What are you doing?" She grasped his shoulders to keep her balance.

"Inspecting you for any further injuries first. Then I shall warm you with my body." He snagged the hem of her wet shift and glanced up at her, passion blazing in his eyes. Slowly, he lifted the hem to her knees. An inspection began, of her bare toes and her calves, his hands gently gliding upward, the hem now bunching over his wrists as he rose. A sweep up and over her hips, his heat caressing every inch of her then he moved in behind her, whispered in her ear, "Arms up."

Stretching her arms high, he drew her shift over her head, his body cocooning hers from behind. He dropped her shift and it fell with a wet *plop* to the floor, his hands now skimming her back and sides. "There are a few yellowish marks on your skin."

"Bruises from the kidnapping. They're easing."

"I'm so sorry for all that's happened to you." Easing back in front of her, he cupped her breasts, flicked his thumbs over both stiff nipples, the pink flesh of her areola wrinkled tight from the cold. With his head dipped, he suctioned his mouth around first one nipple then the other. Moving back and forth, he suckled her nipples, the warm wetness of his tongue sending tingles flaring out from the tips.

"I've longed for this moment since we were parted."

She grasped his sword belt and unbuckled it. "One of us is overdressed, which would be you, *Amati.*"

"Allow me." He divested himself of his weapons, saber and daggers, then he loosened the laces of his damp white tunic, pulled it over his head and dropped it at his feet. Boots toed off, he shoved his breeches down his muscled legs and off. His silky black hair dripped water on his shoulders, the drops trailing down his smooth sun-kissed skin, his chest muscles flexing and biceps bulging.

Her breath came harder and faster, the rigid length of his cock saluting her high from a nest of black curls. She wrapped her hand around his shaft, his body hot, his masculine scent fresh. "Watching you undress is invigorating."

"I'm desperate for you." He released a splurge of Italian, all gruff and huskily spoken, then he returned to English. "I have never wanted a woman the way I want you."

"Your feelings are reciprocated." She squeezed his cock, not too hard and not too soft, which he seemed to like since he captured her mouth and took her breath away with a passionate kiss. Suddenly, he was lifting her, dropping her onto his bed and she landed on his soft quilt with her legs splayed and one of his knees between her knees. He nudged her legs farther apart, caressed along her inner thighs.

"I'm not sure how gentle I can be." He pushed one finger deep inside her channel, his sapphire eyes blazing like blue-fire, then he removed his finger and lowered his powerful body down on top of hers, their legs entwined and his cock stiff against her belly.

Her heart pounded to a frantic beat at having him so close, her inner channel hot and wet and needy for his finger again. She ached to have his mouth on hers once more. "Anteros, please, *baciami*?"

"I love it when you speak Italian to me." He kissed her, his lips firm then going silky soft with the gentlest of caresses. This man was so big and strong and all hers. As he feasted at her mouth, she itched for more, desire swarming her senses.

"You must teach me some more sinful words that I can speak to you, only you." She embraced the raw intimacy of the moment, one she never wished to halt. Pressing her breasts against his chest, she hooked her arms around his neck, wrapped her legs around his hips and accepted every one of his ravishing kisses and loving nips.

"Your desire for passion inflames my own." Cupping one breast, he sucked and moaned around the hardening tip. "You have the sweetest nipples. I dream of laying my head between your breasts at night and devouring them for hours upon hours."

"Kiss them both." She scooped her breasts together.

Holding her gaze, he lapped at her breasts and shards of pleasure rippled through her with each hot stroke of his tongue. "Like so?" he asked mischievously.

"Yes, exactly like so." Arching into his mouth, she floated away on a dreamy storm of sensations.

"I need to taste more of you." He shuffled down, suddenly hooked her legs over his shoulders and settled himself directly between her thighs, her bottom lifting from the bed and her womanhood fully exposed to him. "*Dolce amore mio,* you have the prettiest pink flesh, so lush and just waiting for me to taste it."

"You can't mean to—"

"Yes, I do." He plunged his finger deep inside her again, then he pumped as he captured her nub between his lips. Like a man starved, he sucked madly at her womanhood. She bucked, almost losing her mind, the pleasure of his mouth on her completely sublime. He groaned her name, added a second finger then circled both fingers deep inside her.

Heat built, hard and sharp. Clawing his shoulders, she whimpered and writhed against his wicked tongue. "Anteros, let me touch you too." She wanted to give him the same intense pleasure he currently bestowed on her.

"I'm coming. I desperately need your touch too." He released her legs, lifted up and grasped her hand. He curled her fingers around his hard shaft and helped her pump him with a tight hold. "That's how I like it. Keep working me, while I return to touching you below and kissing your sweet mouth."

His mouth descended on hers, his tongue dipping between her lips and his fingers plunging deep inside her channel below. He circled his thumb over her nub and she cried out as he took her swiftly over the edge.

Blissful spasm after spasm shook her body, then he shook too in her hand, his seed jetting from him in one hot pulse after another. With a guttural groan, he sank against her, his heady presence filling her with such sweet comfort. She held onto him, fingernails digging into his shoulders and her lips near his ear. "*The cobra* has struck. I feel gloriously weak."

"You're so beautiful, so responsive." His voice was

filled with emotion. "But I must be getting too heavy for you."

"Don't go anywhere." She clutched him tighter, adoring his heaviness.

"One moment, *Amore*." Sliding one hand underneath her bottom, he kept her pinned close as he rolled them over until she came up on top of him, his arms banded tight about her. "That is better, hmm?"

"Yes, this is exactly where I need to be." Eyes closed, she cuddled into him, this man the only one her heart and soul ached for. Contentment warmed her through, the dark of the night taking her away into blissful sleep.

Chapter 17

The dawn sun shimmered into his cabin as Anteros stirred the next morning. Olivia lay curled on her side in front of him, her bare bottom snug in the curve of his groin and the humid air of the Mediterranean breezing through his partially open window. His woman was such a temptress. He'd loved her once more during the night when she'd awoken in alarm at her strange surroundings. When she'd seen his face in the moonlight, she'd quickly calmed and broken into a heart-melting smile before kissing him with ravishing abandon. They'd ended up in a sweaty tangled heap as he brought her to a raucous climax, two of his fingers buried deep in her channel where he wanted to bury his cock instead.

"Anteros?" Olivia rolled onto her back and stretched, her arms rising and her beautiful breasts bobbing free as the covers slid away to her waist. When she blinked her eyes open and gave him a sultry-eyed look, every ounce of blood in his body bolted straight to his cock and hardened it.

"You need your rest after I kept you up all night long. Go back to sleep." He shoved his pillow over his crotch currently tenting the bedsheet. "Ignore that."

"I had no issue with the way you kept me up." Another stretch, her breasts swaying full and heavy and her locket emblazoned with his insignia gleaming between both creamy mounds. Planting a hand on his chest, she pinned him to the mattress, then she straddled his hips and sat on him. "We need to talk."

"About…" He lifted his upper body, licked her rosy nipples.

"Your true identity."

"I'm not talking about that." He fell back against the mattress, her question the last he ever wanted to hear.

"There is a reason why Violet and I couldn't gain our freedom on board The Venture. Bruno carried a letter from Ferdinand III of the Kingdom of Sicily, which stated Bruno's position amongst the king's staff, that he must be shown every courtesy on his return to Sicily or else they would suffer the wrath of the king. I first thought the letter a forgery, but Violet assured me it wasn't. So many things began to make sense if it were the truth. If you were Ferdinand's son. It would also explain why Ferdinand would have such cause as to have Bruno kidnap me and take me away from you. Ferdinand wouldn't have wished to see his grand plans for his son foiled. I am Ferdinand's bait, meant to draw you in so he got his wish, for you to marry the Archduchess Clementina. What I don't understand though, is why either you or Adrestia would hide your true parentage from everyone, particularly me."

"You are very astute." He couldn't continue to keep the truth of his birth from her, not now she'd all but guessed it anyway. Cradling her bare hips, he drew in a deep fortifying breath. "I'm Prince Anteros Carlo from the House of Bourbon. A Prince of Naples and Sicily. Adrestia is a Princess of Naples and Sicily. We have always hidden the truth about our births. To begin with, our parents did so to ensure we survived any attempts at assassination during our younger years. Our parents had lost other children, too many for them not to consider some form of foul play being involved. That is how Adrestia and I came to be born and raised on Paradiso."

She stared at him, not blinking or moving, then she lowered her gaze to his chest, her eyes getting watery before she lifted her gaze back up again. "Your secret would have been safe with me. What do you intend on doing now?"

"I'm going to confront my father. It's clear he instructed Bruno to carry out your abduction. Here I'd thought I was the one instigating a ruse, but all along I've been playing right into Father's hands."

"What will you do during this confrontation?"

"Father holds Sicily, but he lost Naples to our enemy and now wishes to reclaim his kingdom. That's why he is so determined to see me wed Clementina. My marriage to the girl will ensure our ties to Austria remain strong. Father needs Austria on our side when it comes time for him to go into battle for the throne of Naples."

"Can't he get Austria on his side another way?" She leaned closer, her blond locks sweeping like a curtain around them. Morning sunshine streamed through his square-cut windows and caught the fine strands. Her hair shimmered like pure gold, so silky and soft.

"Possibly, but it takes time to forge new alliances, which means he'll have longer to wait. There is also the fact that *possibly* isn't in my father's vocabulary." Which meant he had a decision to make, one that involved the woman in his bed. He needed to ensure her safety, of which only one way seemed clearly obvious—giving into his father's demands. He lifted her from him, swung out of bed and opened the lid of his trunk. "Father has long arms and I'll never be able to keep you safe unless I submit to his wishes and marry the girl."

"You can't marry Clementina, not when you don't love her." She jumped out of bed, her body gloriously nude as she stepped in front of him.

"Love has very little to do with marriage, particularly in my family. Political alliances are what we forge." Firming his resolve, he dressed, donning tan breeches and a loose-sleeved white tunic. "You were under my protection, yet still Bruno managed to kidnap you. I can't take that risk again. Your continued safety means the world to me."

"I wish to stay with you." She poked him in the chest.

"I told you from the beginning I wasn't looking for a wife."

"But it appears you're taking one. I want that wife to be me."

"No." A firm answer. He strapped his saber to his hip and daggers to his wrist and ankle, pulled on a pair of boots and stuffed his pistol down the front of his waistband. "What we've had is an affair. You had physical needs. I had physical needs. We've both eased them."

"Physical needs, my foot. Don't you try and erect a barrier between us, Anteros." She swiped one of his tunics from the pile in his trunk and drew the soft white fabric over her head. It skimmed down her body, past her hips and fell in a swish to her knees. She foraged once more and pulled out his sapphire dressing robe, which she stuck her arms in and belted at her waist, the hem trailing behind her as she stomped to his side table. She nabbed his brush and dragged it through her hair, her golden gaze fierce on him. "You belong to me."

"If I speak vows with Clementina, then you'll no longer be in any danger. My problems will then be solved."

"I can handle your father."

"You don't even know him." He snapped his teeth together. "My parents have taken great pains to make politically advantageous marriages for all of their children. I am no different, even though I'm a lost prince and don't wish to wed. I will speak to Father and inform him that I'll marry the Emperor of Austria's daughter."

"You're giving up on us?"

"I won't allow your life to be placed on the line again. You've survived one kidnapping, but there could well be more if I don't agree to Father's wishes."

"I would make a good wife." She tossed the brush onto the bed, thumped across and slammed her hands on her hips. "I adapt well to changes, would gladly live wherever you sailed to."

"Since your kidnapping, all I've done is lived in fear." Growling low, he stepped her backward until her back came up against the wooden paneled wall. "I cannot, nor will not continue living in such a way, and neither will you."

"So you'd prefer to let me go?"

"My decision is made. My future isn't with you." Time to show her he meant what he said. He swallowed hard, the walls of his cabin closing in on him. "I, ah, as you're aware, I haven't had a woman in a very long time, and I wish to thank you for servicing me."

"Servicing you?"

"*Sì*, servicing me."

She slapped his face.

Chapter 18

Never more infuriated, Olivia stormed from Anteros's quarters to the deck, the sails pulled tight with the wind and the ship skimming the waves. Serving him! Olivia wanted to slap Anteros again. Muttering under her breath, she bustled up the short flight of stairs to the helm where Giovani gripped the wheel. "Excuse me, but I would like to speak to Adrestia. Can you bring the ships together?"

"Adrestia has been asking to speak to you too. I'll lower the sails so she can board The Cobra. You look angry. Is everything all right?"

"No. Adrestia now please." Curt words, which made her feel bad. Giovani didn't deserve her anger, only Anteros did.

"Of course." He waved to Adrestia sailing alongside them. "Lower the sails," he bellowed.

"Will do." A wave back from Adrestia and a few minutes later both ships bobbed in the water as Giovani set a plank in place between the two vessels.

Dressed in ruby breeches and a loose tan tunic, her black locks flying free, Adrestia stepped across and jumped onto the foredeck beside her. A hug and a kiss to both her cheeks. "My sweet *sorella*. How are you this fine morning?"

"Upset. Angry. Distressed." She gritted her teeth, the smooth fabric of Anteros's sapphire silk dressing robe blowing about her legs like a lover's caress. "Your brother is the most insufferable man I've ever met."

"Oh, what has he done now?" Her friend grasped her shoulders, her frown fierce. "Tell me, and I'll slay him for you."

"He told me he now intends on marrying the Emperor of Austria's daughter, the stupid lout. I also guessed the truth about the secret you two share. I promise to never speak a word about it to anyone else. Of course, Violet also knows, but she'd never repeat it either." She crossed her heart. "I give you my word."

"I know you'd never speak of it. Good grief, but he cannot marry Clementina." Adrestia released a torrent of Italian before muttering, "My brother has many faults, but never would I have believed him capable of choosing to surrender to Father's wishes. We have retrieved you safely. That is all that matters."

"He has made his decision, which apparently, I must simply abide by." Wracking pain tore through her. She gripped the railing, the choppy swell splashing the side of the ship, the waters as turbulent as her current emotions. "He fears for my life. I understand that, but still, I need to change his mind, only I've no idea how."

"When Bruno first kidnapped you, he told me what

173

Shira warned him about." Adrestia laid a gentle hand on her shoulder, her voice lowering as two rescued passengers strolled past. "The seer proclaimed that his angel would be both the intervention and the prevention of his death, that he must keep you at his side, at all times, day and night, whether he is on English soil or sailing the dangerous waters he knows so well. If he chooses the Austrian girl, then he'll be ignoring that warning. Not a wise decision."

"Shira. Perhaps if I speak to her too, she might be able to offer me some much-needed advice." Hope bloomed in her heart. "I wish for her to read my future. Is that possible?"

"Hmm, well Algiers is only a half day's sail away." Adrestia motioned to the south across the glittering blue waters of the Mediterranean, her brow wrinkling in clear consideration of her request.

"Please, you must take me to see her. I'm not sure what else I can do. You know how stubborn your brother can be." She also couldn't get to Algiers without Adrestia's aid. "I love him. I can't lose him."

"He's in love with you as well, not that he'll admit it." Her friend rubbed her arm. "Algiers isn't exactly a safe place for us to visit. Father has spies there, men who will report back to him about our comings and goings."

"Adrestia is right." Giovani stepped in beside them, while over his shoulder on the upper deck Anteros now stood at the helm, his gaze narrowed on her, the wind rushing through his shoulder length black hair and blowing it about.

"It is Shira who first told Anteros that he would meet me, his angel. I wish to hear what she now says about my future." If she had both Adrestia and Giovani agreeing to her request, then Anteros couldn't argue against all three of them quite so easily. Or at least she hoped that was the case. "Can't we sneak in while it's dark?"

Adrestia tapped her chin, her gaze thoughtful. "We could drop anchor at the very edge of the Bay of Algiers and then have Shira brought to you." She glanced at Giovani. "It's worth the risk if we can get further guidance for Olivia. I want my brother to be happy, and he'll never be happy with Clementina."

"Only under the complete fall of night, and only if Olivia remains below deck." Giovani eyed her. "If the spies reported back about seeing you, then Ferdinand would know Bruno had failed in his attempt to bring you to him."

"I promise to remain below deck." Giddily, she kissed Giovani and Adrestia's cheeks. "Thank you, both of you. I'm forever grateful for your aid."

"Giovani and I would do anything for you. You are family, *Sorella*. You always have been, and always will be." Adrestia caught her flapping dressing robe belt and added, "I also should have considered you would need clothing this morning. Violet too. Come on board my ship. I have plenty of garments you can choose from in my cabin. You certainly cannot continue to wear my brother's robe about the ship."

"I will take you up on your kind offer."

"Good morning, everyone." Violet skipped in beside her wearing lad's clothing, fawn breeches and a loose pale blue tunic, her glossy brown curls fluttering free. "I borrowed some of Wills' clothing. Did you sleep well, my friend?"

"Very well." She embraced Violet, squeezing her a little too tight before releasing her. "We're both free again."

"I've an apple for ye, Lady Olivia." Wills arrived with a cherry whistle. He pulled a red-skinned apple from his coat pocket, polished it against one woolen sleeve and handed it to her. "I pinched this from the cook's galley. The cap'n has arranged a meal for him and ye to be served on the upper deck shortly, but this will tide ye over until then."

"Thank you, Wills, although please inform the captain I've no desire to eat with him. You may take my place, if you please." She bit into the sweet apple and chewed. Another bite, then she hooked an arm through Violet's arm. "Adrestia has offered to share some clothing from her wardrobe. Are you attached to those breeches, or would you like a gown?"

"A gown please."

"Giovani, aid the ladies to my ship. They have gowns to choose." Adrestia bounded onto the plank, effortlessly and gracefully. "Who shall be first?"

Violet raised a hand and Giovani boosted her up and guided her across the thick plank, then once he had Violet settled on Adrestia's deck, he strolled back to her and extended a hand. She finished off her apple, tossed the core into the sea and holding Wills' shoulder for support, clambered up onto the railing in a rather undignified way, her robe swishing open to her knees, the trailing ends of it snagging on the plank. She wobbled and Anteros was suddenly there, right behind her on the plank, his hands on her hips as he held her steady.

She ignored him as best as she could, her anger at him

still thrumming strongly. She reached for Giovani who gallantly steered her across. Adrestia and Violet had already disappeared below deck, so she hurried to catch up with them.

"Wait one moment, Lady Olivia!" Anteros called from the plank where he stood, his booted feet set wide and one hand curled around the hilt of his belted saber. The breeze puffed out his white tunic, billowing the sleeves and plastering the front against his muscled chest. He appeared every inch the captain he was, a man born to lead, a man also born a prince.

How had she not seen the truth until now? What with his regal bearing and plethora of men who jumped to carry out his bidding. Such loyal friends and a loyal crew. No doubt everyone around her knew the truth. As he touched his reddened cheek holding her palm print, a spasm of guilt washed through her. "I apologize for striking you."

"No, I'm the one who should be apologizing, not you." Remorse lined his face. "I never should have spoken to you the way I did, and I sincerely apologize and ask for your forgiveness."

Two of his crew scaling the rigging behind him halted their climb. It would have been impossible for them not to have heard their captain's apology, although they quickly continued on.

"You're forgiven." Papa had always taught her to forgive another when they were truly remorseful, and she'd always done so. Forgiving him though didn't mean forgetting.

"Please, change your mind and join me at the helm to break your fast." A clear plea in his tone. "The cook is preparing a few Sicilian treats for us. Have you ever eaten *arancine*? They're Sicilian rice balls filled with ham and cheese. The cook deep fries them, then serves them with his flavorsome pesto sauce. It is *delizioso*. Will you join me?"

"No, I must sadly decline." Not the answer she wanted to give him, but perhaps he needed a taste of what life might be like without her. "You're soon to marry another lady and it wouldn't be right if I commandeered your attention when it now clearly belongs to another. Good day, Captain Bourbon."

He released a plethora of Italian then growling low under his breath, bounded down from the plank and stormed toward her. When he halted in front, he growled some more. "I need you within my sight," he muttered.

"Why would that be?" She offered him her politest smile, her arms crossed and one bare foot tapping the deck.

"Because it feels damn wrong when you're not."

"Are you saying you hold feelings for me?"

"Yes. No." Another growl.

"Which answer is it to be?"

"We are friends. We've been friends for a long time."

"Anteros, I can't be your friend anymore, not after our affair, and quite honestly, I don't wish to be enticed back to your ship. I think it would be best if I stayed right here with Adrestia until we reach Paradiso. When we part, it'll be far easier for us both. Don't you agree?"

"No, I don't agree. Your reasoning is completely unrealistic."

"Then are you saying that you've allowed your fears for me to rise and in doing so, now condemned yourself to a future with a lady you don't wish to wed? Tell me that's the truth, that you'll set her aside and choose me instead. If you do, I'll join you."

He remained stubbornly quiet, his eyes darkening to a turbulent blue.

"You've nothing to say?" Another tap of her foot.

"I am the dark, and you are the light. That is the truth between us, the only truth that matters."

"Well, here's some more truth then. Adrestia has promised to take me to Algiers. I intend on asking Shira to read my future. I will then follow her advice, whatever that advice happens to be. I've certainly had enough of being stepped on by you. It isn't as if I can't find myself a husband who will appreciate me for who I am. I've received a number of proposals in the past year and a half since we first met, but each one I've turned down because of my feelings for you. I shan't do so again with the next proposal I receive, no matter who it comes from." She motioned to Giovani who coiled a rope on board The Cobra. "If Giovani proposed to me right now, I would accept his offer. That is how serious I am about the issue."

"Giovani will lose his tongue if dares to utter a proposal to you."

"I will even accept Baron Herbarth's offer of marriage. In fact, I will seek him out on my return to England and beg him to marry me. Handsome Lord Herbarth." She sighed with great exaggeration. "Have I mentioned he has an entrancing singing voice? So easy to listen to."

"Like hell you'll marry him." An angry scowl, his voice echoing across the deck. "You truly wish to marry a greedy, pompous ass simply to prove a point to me?"

"Mind your language, sir. You are speaking of my

soon-to-be future husband." She turned and walked away, but not without one last parting shot over her shoulder. "At least he has been more honest with me than you have to date."

Goodness, that felt good to let her emotions out. It also felt far too good watching him squirm and fume. With a jaunty step, she walked down the companionway and once below deck, followed the excited chatter of Adrestia and Violet's voices up ahead. She entered a spacious cabin with a large bed covered in burgundy and gold covers, a wingchair upholstered in the same richly-appointed fabric gracing one corner. Violet twirled about in a forest-green day gown with long sleeves and full skirts.

Adrestia clapped. "Oh Violet, that color suits your completion to perfection."

"You have my immense thanks for the loan of this gown." Violet dropped onto the end of the bed with a puff of her skirts, matching forest-green slippers adorning her twiddling toes as she kicked her feet up. "It is so wonderful to be free again."

"Come in, come in. Don't linger in the doorway, *Sorella*." Adrestia grasped her hand and tugged her toward her tall-standing wardrobe fixed against one wall. Rustling through the selection of gowns hanging within, her friend murmured, "Let's see. For you I would choose a snowy-white velvet since you are my brother's *angelo*. Here we are, the perfect choice. This day gown is a match to that color and has a short train at the back with dainty yellow flowers embroidered along the hem. Do you like it?"

"It is beautiful. Thank you." She accepted the gown then hugged it to her chest, the fabric soft and smooth as she stroked the plush velvet, the sleeves short and puffy.

"The cabin directly across the passageway from mine is yours. Once you've changed, join us out on the deck. Violet and I will be at the helm." Adrestia handed her a clean chemise and a pair of white silk slippers. "We will leave for Algiers shortly."

"That sounds perfect." She left them and opened the door to her new room for the night, her friends stepping into the passageway and wandering toward the stairs, their chatter ringing back to her. She closed the door to her new accommodations and leaned back against it. A large bed with yellow and white striped bedcovers dominated the room, a canopy of sheer yellow netting that could be pulled down at night, lay draped over the top. A basin and jug sat on a corner stand, the window opened a notch and fresh sea air wafting through.

She wandered about, tracing a finger along the windowsill. Out the window, Anteros's ship bobbed in the waters, while a seagull squawked overhead then flew down and landed on the edge of The Cobra's crows' nest. Beady-eyed, the bird surveyed the deck for any forgotten crumbs left by the crew. She was much like that seagull, a bird holding onto a perch and awaiting whatever crumbs Anteros might throw to her. Well, not anymore. If he couldn't understand that they were far stronger together than they'd ever be apart, then he'd soon be losing her. Such an obstinate man.

After divesting herself of Anteros's sapphire robe and tunic, she slid a wonderfully clean chemise over her head then wriggled into the glorious gown she'd borrowed, the high waist lifting her breasts and the skirts flaring to her ankles. She tugged on the matching white slippers and swished from the cabin.

She emerged on deck and—

"*Angelo*?" Anteros leaned against the wall she'd passed, his gaze dipping to her low neckline where the upper swells of her breasts rose.

"You gave me a fright." She patted her racing heartbeat. "I thought you would have returned to your ship."

"You seem to have already wound Giovani and Adrestia around your finger. I have passengers to deliver to Sicily. Diverting to Algiers first will mean a longer trip for them."

"Not by much." She stepped up to him and he lurched forward, clutched her hips and gave a tug. She lost her balance, got plastered against him, then the annoying man nuzzled her neck, nipped her skin. "There are passengers who might see us." A few strolled the deck.

"You're right. I've already commandeered a secluded spot at the stern where we can eat without interruption, in complete privacy. No passengers or crew about." He scooped her into his arms and stalked toward the rear of the ship.

"Put me down, Anteros. I'm not eating with you." She crossed her arms, one elbow jabbing into his chest.

"Since you declined eating on board my ship, I've brought the food to you. There's hot chocolate, which I know you adore." He was ignoring every single word she said. Up a short flight of stairs, he jogged, then into an alcove set with a table and two chairs. A cozy arrangement offering complete privacy. "If you eat with me, we will sail to Algiers and I will collect Shira myself and bring her to your cabin."

"Put me down."

"As you wish." He settled her on her feet, pulled out a chair. "Sit."

"You are being overbearing and obnoxious." Since her belly rumbled, giving away her need for food, she eased into the seat and he tucked her in closer to the table before pulling out the second chair and seating himself.

"I've never professed to having manners, remember?"

"I'm looking forward to meeting Shira." She ignored his last comment.

"The last time Shira and I spoke, she told me to bring you to her. She wishes to meet you." Grinning like a wolf who'd gotten his way, he scooped a fried rice ball with his fingers, smeared it through the pesto sauce and held it to her lips. "I cannot wait to share some food from my homeland with you. These delicate morsels are eaten from one's fingers. Open your mouth, *Amore*. Let me feed you."

She gave in a little, opened her mouth.

He popped the succulent rice ball between her lips and she closed her mouth on his fingers and swiped the sauce from his fingertips with her tongue. She chewed, while he stared at her mouth in complete fascination.

"I'm an idiot for letting you go," he mumbled. "I know I am, but that is how it must be."

"You terrify me sometimes." With her heart in her throat, her voice barely above a whisper, she continued, "You pull me toward you, push me away, then pull me back again."

"I do no such thing." He popped a rice ball into his

mouth, the air fairly crackling with tension between them.

"Anteros, I've never experienced this kind of bond with anyone else. Only with you. What we have goes beyond friendship, beyond passion, and dare I say it, even beyond destiny. No matter where you sail, I want to stand beside you, but if you're not willing to accept what I'm offering then we're both going to end up adrift on the sea, always wishing we could have had what we're about to lose." She looked deep into his eyes and caught the flare of pain etched in his own. "You detest fighting with me, the same way I detest fighting with you."

"*Baciami?*" He pushed his chair back, held out one hand.

She rose from her chair and stepped in between his thighs. Gently, she pushed her fingers deep into his silky black hair and when she met his gaze, she couldn't miss the intense emotions swirling within his eyes. Loneliness. Need. Want. "Anteros, you need a wife who will be your companion, who will sail these seas with you. Of course you have your sister and Giovani, but they are not enough. You need a family of your own, children who will clamber up the masts and swing about the sails. You need me."

"I don't want children." Yet that loneliness intensified. He caught her hips and buried his face against the flatness of her belly, then slowly he kneaded her hips through the snowy-white velvet of her gown. "I don't want a wife either."

"Whatever am I going to do with you?" She lifted his face to hers, pressed a soft kiss against his forehead, then each cheek before settling her mouth over his mouth. She kissed him, long and deep, then she teased the tip of her tongue over his tongue and lost herself in the passion he always brought rising swiftly to the surface within her.

"Cap'n!" An excited shout as Wills bounded up the stairs and skidded in beside them, a wide smile splitting his face. "The wind is rising. Giovani says he can't keep the ships hooked together for much longer. Do we sail for Algiers?"

"We do. Tell him I'll be there directly." A firm nod from Anteros, and the boy sprinted off.

"Go," she murmured as she stepped back from him. "We can speak again later."

He rose, dipped in and stole another heated kiss from her before he strode away.

Chapter 19

Several hours later as they neared the Bay of Algiers, Anteros stood at the helm of his ship, the sun skimming the horizon, half sunken and its magnificent glow sending a final spear of orange-red bleeding into the twilight-blue. A few stars appeared, twinkling here and there as he rounded the tip and entered the bay. Ahead, the citadel rose like a sentinel along the land, guarding the desert sands rising high behind it.

Flanking him on the water, Adrestia sailed in tandem with him, while Olivia stood at the curve of The Decadence's bow, his woman so close yet also so far away. With her elbows resting on the railing, the night wind blew her hair back like a golden sail, her snowy-white skirts billowing about her slim legs, legs she'd wrapped around him just last night. Hell, she was the only woman who'd ever truly seen right through the façade he always donned. How on earth was he supposed to let her go when all he wanted to do was tie her to his side and ensure she never escaped him again?

He handed the wheel to Giovani and jogged to the bow of his ship, the distance now between him and Olivia only twenty or thirty feet. "It's time for you to be out of sight," he called to her.

"Of course. I'll go below deck now." She grasped her skirts and weaved around the sailors on deck, then when she reached the stairs leading down into the companionway, she snuck a look back at him, clear longing evident in her beautiful golden eyes.

Likely the same longing that shimmered in his own eyes.

Blast it all, he was such a fool.

A lost fool whose heart pined for a woman he couldn't have, not if he wanted to keep her safe. As she disappeared, he dragged his gaze back to the fortified walls of Algiers.

The night sky now covered them like a shimmering blanket of black. Time to drop anchor. He gave the order, Adrestia doing the same, their vessels indistinguishable now from any other vessel out on the water.

Since he'd already formulated a plan with Adrestia and Giovani, he followed through and met his right-hand man at starboard where Giovani lowered a skiff over the side of the ship. They would fetch Shira and bring her back to the ship to speak to Olivia here, where she would be the safest.

"Be careful, *Fratello*." Adrestia blew him a kiss from her vessel, her voice floating to him over the water.

"I always am." He wrapped a black headdress around his head to keep his identity hidden as best as he could, then clambered down the roped netting and joined an equally veiled Giovani in the skiff. Seated on the center bench seat, he gripped the oars and rowed them toward shore. Skin damp and his heartbeat thumping madly, he sent a quick prayer skyward for their continued safety this night.

"Shira already awaits us." Giovani motioned toward the shore. "Eastern end of the beach. Change course a little."

"It is at times like these when her ability astounds me." Shira stood alone, leaning against a craggy rock wall near the shore. As the waves rolled into the sandy beach, he guided their skiff in, bounded into the knee-deep surf and jogged toward Shira while Giovani remained with the skiff and turned it around for their return trip back. Grasping the old woman's hands, he murmured, "Have you been well, Shira?"

"Very well, and we shall all be well tomorrow too, *Insha'Allah*."

"That is good to know." Through the slits in his headdress, he quickly searched the beach either side of them. "Are you ready to depart?"

"Yes, take me to your angel, my beloved boy. I have been awaiting this night for a long time. I wish to meet the lady who has seen deep into your soul and wishes to claim you for herself." Shira passed him a basket holding her pots and special brew. "She has many questions for me this night and I pray I shall be able to enlighten her as to the course she now needs to take."

"I need her to return to England." He propped Shira's basket on one hip, took her elbow and guided her to his skiff. Giovani aided Shira in, while he stowed Shira's basket safely in the hull.

"*Marhaba*, Giovani." Shira cupped Giovani's face with her wrinkled hands as she sat beside him. "How are you this night?"

The two chatted away while he pushed the skiff deeper into the water, bounded on board and rowed them back toward The Decadence. He came in alongside Adrestia's roped ladder dangling into the water and taking all care with Shira, aided her up the rigging to the deck. Leaning back toward Giovani with one arm outstretched, he snagged Shira's basket.

"*As-salamu alaykum*, Shira." Adrestia welcomed Shira with a tearful hug. "I have missed you."

"I've missed you too, my sweet girl. You do not come to see me nearly often enough." Shira held Adrestia at arms-length, her gaze sweeping her up and down. "Look at you. You grow more beautiful with each day that passes. The man who will one day be yours will need a great deal of stamina if he wishes to hold onto you."

A giggle from his sister as she hooked Shira's basket over her arm. "Seeing you is a balm to my soul."

"As it is to mine too. Show me to your brother's woman. It is time I met Lady Olivia Trentbury."

"Come with me." Adrestia drew Shira with her toward the stairs leading below deck, the two of them disappearing from his sight.

"Wait here until Shira is ready to return," he called to Giovani over the side, his man still seated in the skiff below. He followed the ladies.

In the doorway of the cabin which Adrestia had given Olivia, the three woman completed introductions then seated themselves on plush pillows before a low table, the bed pushed against one wall to make more room for them.

Shira set to work adding her special coffee to a pot of hot water, then once done with the preparations, she took ahold of Olivia's hand and squeezed it. "You have done well in holding your position with your *emir*."

"*Emir*?" Confusion flickered in Olivia's eyes as she glanced up at him in the doorway. A look back at Shira. "I'm sorry. I'm not aware of what that word means."

"*Emir* is Arabic for prince," Adrestia translated for Olivia.

"Oh I see. I have so many languages I need to learn." Olivia laughed, her smile wide as she beckoned him closer with one finger. "Does my *emir* wish to hear my reading?"

"Only if you wish it, otherwise I will go."

"You should stay. I've already asked Adrestia to remain here."

"Then I'll stay." He closed the door with a quiet snick then eased down onto the low pillow next to hers. Unable to help himself, he lifted her fingers to his lips, his need to touch her as necessary as breathing. He crossed his legs, settled her hand on his right thigh.

She looked into his eyes, hers a little watery.

"Don't cry," he warned with a frown. Otherwise he'd have to take himself to task for upsetting her.

"Let us begin, for there is too much danger about this night for us to dally." Shira swirled the coffee pot and the rich and exotic fragrance of her special blend permeated the air. She poured Olivia a cup and encouraged, "Drink it, my child."

Olivia sipped from the tiny cup and once she'd finished, handed it back to Shira.

Shira spilled the remains onto a saucer and studied the markings she saw. Her azure eyes glowed as she traced her wrinkled fingers around the edge of the saucer. With a deep breath, she lifted her gaze to Olivia. "You must pay heed to my words. Your life has reached a fork in the road. If you choose the pathway to the west you will marry a man you do not love. If you choose to follow the pathway to the east, then you must learn that when your *emir* says no, you must say yes. He will insist he knows best, but his fate is already sealed and now lies in your hands. Spread your wings and fly, my child. You were never meant for any other, not when you've always belonged to him."

Shira struck an equally intense look at him. "I speak now to you, *Emir*. Never forget the words I spoke to you the last time we were together. It's time for you to leave the dark behind and enter into the light. You must accept your new future and allow it to flow into complete alignment with your angel's. You'll never regret doing so, provided you cleave unto her, embracing all that you can be together."

"My angel is fighting for her life right now." A snort under his breath. "She wouldn't be if I'd remained far away from her in the first place."

"My beloved boy, deep in your heart you know you can't live without her. Fight for your future with her." Shira squeezed his arm. "When one finds such a great love as you two have, they should never let it go."

"He is very stubborn," Olivia stated, her voice breathy.

"Yes, but he is your stubborn man." Shira cast a warning look at him. "Your father awaits you. Fight fair but fight well."

Chapter 20

On board The Decadence, Olivia sat on the end of her bed while Anteros paced back and forth in her cabin. Giovani had seen Shira safely back to shore, then they'd set sail. The ship rocked as they continued east toward Sicily, Giovani captaining Anteros's ship since he'd chosen to remain here with her following her reading. With the hour incredibly late, she picked up the pillows scattered on the floor and dropped them onto her mattress, then in her chemise, climbed into bed. With just the bedsheet covering her, the heat far too oppressive for anything heavier, she patted the other side. "Come and lie beside me, *Amati*."

"We need to talk about Shira's reading." He unstrapped his sword belt, pulled his pistol from the front of his tan breeches and placed his weapons on the side table. Boots toed off, he pulled his loose-sleeved white tunic over his head and with his breeches still on, eased down next to her. A thump of the pillow as he settled his head on it.

She settled back too, her gaze on the planked ceiling above, candlelight playing pretty prisms of light over it. "Let's talk about the direction I should take in the fork of the road. To the west lies a man I could marry but who I do not love. Shira must be referring to whom awaits me in England should I return there without you." She rolled onto her side and faced him. "Then there is the east, where you are, where Paradiso lies. Should I travel east—which I currently am—then I must learn that when my *emir* says no, I must say yes. Would you like to argue against any of those points thus far?"

"I can't," he muttered, his covered legs stretched and feet crossed at the ankle, the gold medallion at his neck gleaming. "Which I find incredibly frustrating."

"I particularly liked it when Shira said your fate is already sealed and now lies in my hands." She lifted her locket and rubbed the engraving—so soothing.

"You would." He rolled toward her, his expression studious.

"It's time for you to leave the dark behind and enter into the light, Anteros. You must accept your new future and allow it to flow into complete alignment with your angel's." She repeated Shira's reading word for word. "You'll never regret doing so, provided you cleave unto her, embracing all that you can be together."

A groan as he scrunched his eyes shut.

She caught a lock of his hair falling over his brow and tucked it back. "Do you want to fight for a future with me? As Shira said, 'When one finds such a great love as we have, they should never let it go.'"

"I need time to think this all through."

"Well, while you're busy thinking, I'm going to begin cleaving unto you." Naughtily said as she pushed the bedsheet back and unbuttoned the front flap of his breeches. A shuffle of the fabric down, his cock springing out at her. Meeting his gaze, she grinned. "Can I kiss you here the same way as you kissed me below last eve?"

"Only if you want to." His eyes begged for her to say yes.

"Oh, I want to. Desperately." Slowly, ever so slowly, she took his shaft in hand, bent and pressed a sweet kiss to the flared head. When he shuddered, a bead emerging and glistening on the head, she lifted her gaze to his. "What do I do now?"

"Don't be afraid to take me fully in your mouth. Suck on me. My cock will love every bit of attention you bestow upon it." He caught the sides of her chemise and dragged it over her head, tossed it aside.

A swipe of her tongue and she collected that bead then eyes closing, she rolled his taste over in her mouth. Mmm, slightly sweet, slightly salty, although she'd hadn't taken enough of a taste. More. She needed more. She wrapped her mouth fully around his flared head and sucked strongly. He cupped her face in his hands as she worked her mouth up and down his length, taking him as deep as possible before pulling back and going shallow. More of his essence coated her tongue, which she greedily devoured, her nipples beading tight with desire.

"Damn, that feels so good." A heavy rumble in his chest, his eyes rolling back.

She pumped him with one hand, the other smoothing over his balls which had tightened and drawn up. More sucking. More essence. She soaked in his strength and his taste.

"*Amore*, I'm going to come in your mouth if I don't stop you right now." He pulled back from her, his shaft so incredibly thick, the head darkening to a deep purple.

"I hadn't finished."

"I can't take any more."

"I want everything you have to offer."

"I can't offer you anything at all, not when my father is determined in his endeavor to keep us apart. I can't stand guard over you every hour of every day. Doing so is impossible. Do I need to remind you of how Bruno managed to tear you away from me as evidence?"

"I'm not choosing any other pathway, other than the one which leads directly toward you."

"You are a stubborn woman."

"You are a stubborn man." She scrambled on top of him, straddled his thighs, his cock waving high from the dark nest of curls surrounding it. Rising to her knees, she wrapped her hand around his shaft and rubbed the plump head back and forth against her own slick folds.

"What are you doing?" He moaned, long and low. "This position is extremely distracting for me, Olivia."

"You are like a fine Italian wine, *Amati*. To understand all the characteristics and complexities of who you are, one must consider that wine and the diverse soil of the ground where the grapes for the wine were grown. Could the roots of the vines have been planted deep within the fields of Naples or Sicily, or on an island where the soil is rich from the love and labor of your grandfather?"

"My roots were planted and sustained on Paradiso."

He squeezed her breasts, his thumbs grazing her stiffened nipples.

Heat pooled in her core and dampened that place between her legs which throbbed for his touch. "My roots were planted in England and nurtured by the immense love of my parents. Shira is right. It's time for you to cleave unto me, embracing all that we can be together. I wish to bind you to me by becoming one."

"No." He lifted his head from the pillow and suctioned his mouth around her nipple.

"When your *emir* says no"—she arched her back as he continued to suck and she rubbed his cock harder along her lower folds—"you must say yes."

"No."

"Yes." She wriggled and squirmed for more. She needed him terribly, to join them together as one and no more could she wait. She sank down onto his shaft and cried out as pain tore through her, her channel filled to the brim with his thick cock. "Oh goodness, that hurts."

He shuddered underneath her, his eyes closing and sheer ecstasy flaring across his face. "Don't move," he muttered haggardly. "Or I'll come right now, and you'll never get to experience the pleasure which should be yours the first time we come together as one."

"What should I do?" She grasped his hips, his length embedded fully within her, the sight of his shaft disappearing into her body painfully delicious. "I want you, Anteros. How do I make this better?"

"Lean toward me. Kiss me. Don't hold back." She leaned in as he instructed, his cock jerking inside her. "Slowly, *Amore*, slowly. My cock is in heaven and I feel too much."

"I'll go slower." When she got to within an inch of his mouth, he lifted a touch, captured her lips with his and kissed her with breathless hunger. She kissed him just as hungrily back, then gasped as he massaged her breasts and pinched her nipples. Gently, sweetly, he played with her breasts, then he eased one hand down her torso and fondled her nub.

The pain slowly eased, and pleasure began to build.

"Lift up a little, then settle back down on me." Whispered words against her lips, his fingers still working their wonderful magic over her below.

She lifted up as he instructed, sank again, her breasts swaying in his hands.

He tweaked one nipple, the rosy tip arching toward him for more of his pleasurable touch. "Continue to move up and down on me, until you feel more comfortable being seated on top."

"Am I doing this right?" She followed his instructions, exposing part of his shaft again, then she closed her eyes as she eased back down. Less pain this time. Slowly up again, higher this time, then down. Tingles radiated out, his cock suddenly hitting a spot inside her which spurred even more pleasure to flow.

"Did that feel better?" he asked around her breast, his mouth divine on her flesh.

"Yes."

"Higher, Olivia. Go higher and expose more of me."

She exposed almost all of his shaft, only a fierce sense of loss flared through her and she sank back down on him, right to the hilt. No pain this time, only a fierce wave of pleasure as heat spiraled through her. "Oh my, this I like."

"You're so responsive." He dragged his mouth along her neck and nipped at her fluttering pulse point. "Maintain a rhythm, as if you were atop your horse and enjoying a ride."

"I love riding." Back arched, she did as he instructed, her breath quickening.

"Do you like being on top of me now?" His hands were everywhere, exploring her body, touching her breasts and her hips and sweeping around to her bottom. He squeezed her lower cheeks as she sank fully down on him.

"Mmm, oh yes, and you feel incredible now inside of me." Hands planted on the pillow either side of his head, she gave into the carnal pleasure flowing through her, his fingers returning to her nub as he caressed with an exquisite stroke. "Please, don't stop touching me." Happiness bubbled inside her, her smile no doubt wicked as she looked into his eyes. "I believe I shall enjoy riding you, Your Highness, as often as I possibly can."

"*Santo Michele.*" He suddenly gripped her hips, lifted her then dropped her back down on top of him even harder.

With her breasts thrust out, she built her pace, rocking his cock deep inside her, then as she found her favored gait, she reached behind her and caressed his balls. He broke into a spiel of Italian, which made her grin. "I love it when you speak like that to me."

An anguished groan.

"I'm about to fly." A wave of heat blazed through her core and washed over her. Her channel tightened, her body shaking, and when he flicked her nub and thrust higher, his cock hammering into the heart of her, she rocketed to the stars.

"You're my *angelo*, always mine," he muttered as he flipped her onto her back and thrust to the hilt, his seed jetting in hot pulses deep inside her.

"Yes, and you're my *emir*, always mine." Pure joy consumed her.

Chapter 21

The next afternoon, following their visit to the port in Sicily where they unloaded their passengers and ensured Violet had safe passage to her palazzo, Anteros finally caught sight of Paradiso directly ahead. Standing at the bow of Adrestia's ship with Olivia in front of him, he held her close as she pressed her back against his chest, her golden locks fluttering across his cheek. He was home, after being gone for far too long, his *castello* rising high on the blustery point ahead and the curve of sand before it shimmering a white-gold in the late afternoon sun. Waves splashed one rock wall and sprayed with a shimmering array of colors, the sky above a warm blue with only a smattering of cloud here and there. He hugged his woman closer, rubbed his chin over the top of her head.

"It is a beautiful castle." Olivia turned in his arms, her rose-colored gown matching the sweet flush of happiness in her cheeks, her smile tearing his heart in two. "A stronghold fit for a prince."

"Yes." He kissed the tip of her nose. "We're stronger together than we'll ever be apart."

"Say that again." A twinkle in her eyes. "Because it sounded suspiciously as if Captain Anteros Bourbon just consigned himself to the truth?"

"You have strengths where I have weaknesses, and I have strengths where you have weaknesses. We balance each other." He'd spent his entire life considering how to live it, never once envisioning a woman at his side, or at least not until she'd entered his life. Love. He'd been fighting that all-consuming emotion since the day he'd first met her. Ruthlessly, he'd tried to control his feelings, except Olivia kept busting down his walls and ensuring he couldn't rebuild them. In the past, even setting sail so he could put a divide of distance between them hadn't worked. He'd always returned to her. He'd tangled himself up in her life, wanting her, craving her. Kissing her sweet lips, he murmured, "You are my whole world."

"I love you," she whispered back.

"This land is my land, will be the land of our children in years to come, but first I must defend it and you against the one man who continues to stand in my way." He kissed her softly, reverently, paying homage to his love for her. Slowly, he lowered to one knee, her hand still in his. "Lady Olivia Trentbury, will you do me the greatest honor of marrying me and becoming my wife? Tonight. With Adrestia and Giovani witnessing our vows. There is a priest on the island."

"Yes." She sank to her knees and kissed him.

"You taste of freedom, of purity, and innocence. You taste of all my hopes and dreams fused together into one. I finally feel as if I've left the dark behind and entered into the light," he admitted, his heart overflowing with the love he held for her.

Boom!

A cannon ball shot through the air and sailed over the bow. It slammed into the water and sent seawater washing over them.

He shoved to his feet, pushed Olivia behind him and pulled his telescope from the sheath at his side and lifted the brass tube to his eye. Father sailed his vessel toward them, coming between him and Paradiso, his father's own scope raised to his eye. "Father has seen you. He appears a little angry over the discovery."

"Well, he'll just need to accept that I'm now a part of your life." She seized his arm from behind. "Make sure you tell him that."

"I will." He'd make sure he hammered the truth home.

"What's your order?" Giovani bellowed as he brought The Cobra closer to the bow of The Decadence.

"My father wants a fight, which means we battle this day." To his men on board both warships, he shouted, "Feed the cannons." Slotting his scope away at his hip, he raised one hand and roared, "Fire!"

Cannon fire soared through the air, smoke puffing from the artillery.

"Come with me." He scooped Olivia into his arms and bounded to the upper deck, set her down next to Adrestia at the wheel, and kissed his sister's cheek. "Take me close enough to board."

"Stay alive, *Fratello*."

"I always do, *Sorella*. I have much more to live for

now than ever before." He bounded over the rail and thumped onto the foredeck amongst his crew. "Fire!" he ordered again.

Their cannons rocked the vessel and balls of fire shot across the sea and joined The Cobra's fire which hit Father's deck. Father's ship lurched under the impact of his dual attack.

Fight fair but fight well. Shira's final words to him shimmered through his head.

"Hold," he yelled. Their position was far too close for another bombardment. "Trim the sails! We're boarding."

His sails got roped in as they glided into position. He tossed a grappling hook which caught on a crossbeam along Father's mizzenmast, gave it a jerk to make certain it wouldn't budge then he heaved back and swung out, his white tunic billowing, his crew whistling across and landing with a thump next to him.

"It appears Captain Bourbon has arrived." Tossing his gold embroidered black jacket aside, Father slid his saber free then bounded in, the red sash at his waist flying.

"You fired upon me first. Don't forget that." He swung, their swords clashing, his men bounding into battle against Father's men. Steel rang out loud against steel.

"Where is Bruno?" Father demanded with a jab.

"Buried at sea." He met each of Father's strikes, blow for blow. "You instructed him to kidnap Lady Olivia, then to bring her directly to you here at Paradiso. He told me not to expect Olivia to remain alive for long. Olivia's death was assured if I didn't bow to your wishes and marry Clementina."

"Bruno didn't tell you the full truth." Father swore, a

storm of Italian curses ringing from him. "Yes, I told him to bring Lady Olivia to me, but that he wasn't to harm a hair on her head. The imbecile. I needed her only as bait. When we last spoke, I sensed your feelings for her ran deep. I would never hurt someone you loved. Doing so would only push you farther away from me, which has never, and will never, be my intention."

"I will never allow another of your men to tail me as Bruno did, or to lay a hand on Olivia." With one strategic strike after another, he pushed Father toward the side of the ship nearest Olivia and Adrestia, right where their ships bumped together. No others fought in that spot, which would afford them far more privacy for their current argument.

"Anteros," Father muttered as he slashed. "You're my son, and I want the best for you. You carry my blood, are a Prince of Naples and Sicily, and as such you should be marrying a woman of equal footing. The Archduchess Clementina's father is the Holy Roman Emperor of Austria. He is the King of Hungary and Croatia and Bohemia. Must I go on about her revered parentage?"

"No, I understand Clementina's lineage is strong, but I am in love with Lady Olivia and you will love her too when you meet her. She is the only one who will ever hold my heart, who *will* be my future wife, and the woman who will bear my children. Mark my words, Father, she is mine and I am hers."

"You are so frustrating, and blast it, so damned like me it is incredibly annoying." Father spluttered and retreated. He sheathed his saber, bellowed to his men, "Cease the fighting and leave me to speak to Captain Bourbon alone.

There shall be no more battling this day."

All went quiet on deck, swords lowered, men heaving as they grasped their knees and caught their breath. Anteros nodded at his own men, that they cease and retreat. The men slowly drifted toward the bow, righting overturned barrels and clearing the debris as they afforded them the privacy they needed. A quick look at Adrestia and Olivia clutching the rail. He gave them both a firm nod, then faced Father once more. "Olivia and I shall be speaking vows this night, so if you'd like to attend our wedding ceremony, then you may."

"I wish you were my firstborn, Anteros." Father paced back and forth, looking aggravated and aggrieved. "You would have ousted Napoleon's brother-in-law from Naples and sent Joachim Murat to his grave by now."

"Murat won't be able to hold his position for long. You'll ascend to the throne of Naples again, and provided you accept Olivia and don't force me to raise arms against you once more, I will be fighting by your side when you go into battle. Do I have your agreement?"

A slow nod, then firmer. "Yes, you do. Fighting against you hasn't been pleasant, and I'd rather never do so again. Introduce me to your lady so I might apologize for Bruno's dishonorable behavior. I wish to know this woman who has captured your heart. She has certainly done what no other woman before her has achieved."

Olivia and Adrestia squealed at hearing Father's words, their excitement bubbling over and making him grin too. Grasping Father's shoulder, he drew him to the rail and gestured to Olivia. "Father, meet your future daughter-in-law, the divine and angelic Lady Olivia Trentbury. Lady

Olivia, meet my father, King Ferdinand III of the Kingdom of Sicily."

"Your Majesty." Olivia dipped into an elegant curtsy, then when she rose, added, "In witnessing this battle, I can see exactly whom your son received his fierce and stubborn nature from."

"Unfortunately, I'd say he's even more stubborn than I am." Father dipped his head in acknowledgement. "I truly do wish to apologize for any harm Bruno brought upon you. He wasn't acting under my orders in that regard. Your safety should never have been brought into question during the kidnapping."

"Bruno has already paid for his crimes." Olivia caught Adrestia's hand on the rail and squeezed, his sister quickly squeezing back as she offered his bride-to-be her full support.

"Which is as it should be." Father reached across the gap where the ships rubbed, placed his hand over both Olivia and Adrestia's, his voice low as he continued, "Welcome to the family, Lady Olivia. There are secrets galore for you to keep, but hopefully not for too much longer. Give me plenty of grandchildren and I shall be happy."

"That I will gladly do." She offered his father an endearing smile, then she burst into conversation, as if there hadn't just been an immense battle raging. He didn't doubt his father would soon fall prey to his angel's sweet form of charm, just as he'd done from the very first day he'd met her.

As the sun began to lower over the horizon, he couldn't help but smile. Today was the first day of the rest of his life. It was time to celebrate a new beginning with the woman he loved, with the woman who had always been his. It wasn't a fanciful notion at all. She belonged to him, and he belonged to her.

Love. It had struck even his hardened heart.

Chapter 22

Eight weeks later, Olivia stood high on the grassy hills overlooking La Rocca Dinastia, the clear blue waters of the bay sparkling in the afternoon sunshine, a number of her husband's ships moored in the bay. Exquisite joy and contentment thrummed through her, the man at her back having brought her that immense joy and so much more. Their love had grown from strength to strength these past two months as they'd roamed the island together, her prince having shown her all of his favorite childhood places so she could experience the beauty and magic of his ancestral home just as he had as a child. They'd even sailed with Adrestia to Sicily to attend the Duchess of Genoa's ball at the Royal Palace of Palermo. Violet had been in attendance too, she and Anteros having collected her from her home.

An hour into the evening, Ferdinand had risen from his elevated throne chair within the glittering expanse of the ballroom, called for everyone's attention, then promptly announced to the thousand elaborately attired guests in attendance that his son, Prince Anteros Carlo from the House of Bourbon, a Prince of Naples and Sicily, and his new daughter-in-law, would now be known as the Duke and Duchess of Paradiso, a new title he'd bestowed upon them.

Shocked, she'd swayed in Anteros's tight hold, her husband also openly staring at his father, all while the crowd around them had broken into thunderous applause. That applause had only died down when Ferdinand had raised a hand to quiet the assembled guests. He'd then quickly followed his first announcement by introducing his daughter, Princess Adrestia Maria, to all assembled.

No longer could either brother or sister hide their true identity, but thankfully, they'd both only felt relief and not distress at the unveiling. After Anteros's surprise had eased, her husband had graciously thanked his father for the honor of the title, then swept her into his arms and commandeered every dance of the night with her. Never had she enjoyed herself more. Such an unfolding of truths, the lies finally laid to rest.

On their return to Paradiso, she'd immediately written to Mama and informed her about all that had happened, of which she'd received a response only a few days ago. Mama's letter of reply had been fourteen pages long, each and every single page filled to the brim with Mama's happiness for her.

"You're rather quiet. What are you thinking?" From behind her, Anteros nuzzled her neck, his teeth scraping sensuously over her pounding pulse point, his hands sliding underneath the hem of her cream blouse, his body surrounding hers with such a heavenly heat.

"That this spot on the island is my favorite place of all." The absolute truth.

"Why is that?" Smiling wickedly, he caressed her middle, his fingers brushing along the undersides of her breasts.

Leaning her head back against his shoulder, she swayed against him. "I've adored seeing all this island has to offer, from the beaches and coves to the cliffside caves and sparkling bays. The villagers are a delight, so friendly and caring, and I love riding across the fields and through the valleys, but this place is where you and I first stood as husband and wife as we spoke our marriage vows before the priest."

"I would never forget such a momentous moment." He cupped her breasts, squeezed her nipples.

She rubbed her bottom against the front of his tight-fitting sapphire breeches, right where his erect cock prodded her backside. "Did I tell you that after we spoke our vows, your father whispered in my ear that I must be good to his son? He loves you, Anteros, no matter the difficult path the two of you have traversed over the years."

"He had you kidnapped." A low growl, his chest rumbling against her back. Oh, it appeared her husband still had a few grievances with his father. Not surprising though. A lifetime of issues couldn't be resolved in only two months. It would take time.

"I didn't say he was without fault." Time to distract her husband. She turned and pushed him backward, toward the hidden hollow where they'd spent many afternoons rolling around in a tangle of entwined limbs.

With a wicked grin, he lowered to his knees in the

thick grass and beckoned her with one finger. "*Carissima,* come to me."

"Remove your clothing and I shall."

He stripped, exceedingly fast, his white cravat and shirt disposed of in a soft pile at his feet, his breeches and boots tossed behind him. Holding a make-believe bow and arrow, he winked at her as he drew the arrow back, then released it with a soft *ping.*

"You truly are like the Greek god of love and passion you're named after." She joined him in the hollow, moving to her knees before him, her cream skirts flaring out behind her and sheer happiness overflowing her heart. "You and I were destined to be together, *Amati.*"

"For always and forever, *Amore.*" He unbuttoned her blouse and slipped it over her shoulders, then he loosened the ties of her skirts and allowed the fabric to pool into a gloriously silken mass on the grass.

He toppled her onto the nest of their clothes and the burning began, deep in her core, her need for him an unstoppable beat as it always would be. In a storm of passion and complete harmony, she held him deep inside her body as he joined with her in all ways, his fierce warmth spreading through each and every inch of her.

Together, they'd confronted his father.

Together, they'd won the battle.

Together, they'd fallen endlessly in love.

Anteros plunged inside her, his rigid length going deep, over and over again, and she got swept away, cleaving unto him and embracing all that they could be together as one. Spreading her arms even wider, she soared higher than she'd ever soared before, her prince taking flight right alongside her.

Heaven. This was pure heaven.

As was the baby cradled deep in her belly, the child still a secret she hadn't yet shared with her husband. She intended to now though, in this most precious of places. Holding him close as they both came back down from the heights of ecstasy where they'd flown, she whispered in his ear, "You're going to be a father in another seven months."

"Are you certain?" His cock twitched inside her, suddenly filling again.

"I haven't had my courses since I arrived on this island, so yes, I'm very certain."

"*Ti amo. Ti amo.* I love you." Smile wide, dimples showings, he kissed her thoroughly.

"I love you too." He was her prince, the man she belonged to, the world beyond these shores now theirs to explore together.

Such an incredible adventure awaited them.

She couldn't wait to begin it.

Author's Note – A Must Read

I've had so much fun writing this Regency Brides series. This series is supposed to be five books in length, but I truly feel as if I've only just begun, that there are still so many stories to tell. If you've been with me throughout this journey across all five books, then you'll have read about Captain Bradley Poole who stood at Harry's side during the Battle of Sobral in The Wartime Bride. I long to write his story. I also have the perfect heroine for Christopher Raven, Viscount Avery, from The Earl's Secret Bride. Then there is Adrestia. Oh my, I can only say that I've already had her hero plaguing my dreams with the whirlwind of an adventure the two of them are destined to have.

If you wish for me to write their stories and to continue this series, then please leave a review on this book stating that is so. It is my job to write books for you, and I take that job seriously, so if you make your demands known, I will quickly buckle and obey.

Time to chat about King Ferdinand now. He was known as Ferdinand IV of the Kingdom of Naples, and

Ferdinand III of the Kingdom of Sicily. Ferdinand and his wife did in fact have many children over the course of their marriage, eighteen to be exact, with only seven of the eighteen having survived to adulthood.

Here's some more key information about King Ferdinand. He was deposed twice from the throne of Naples, once by the revolutionary Parthenopean Republic for six months in 1799, and again by Napoleon Bonaparte in 1805. Napoleon replaced Ferdinand with his own brother, Joseph Bonaparte, in 1806. Joseph then ruled Naples for two years before being replaced by Napoleon's brother-in-law, Joachim Murat, in 1808. This story takes place in 1811, when Joachim Murat held the throne.

On the 3rd of March 1815, following the Austrian victory of the Battle of Tolentino, Ferdinand was once more restored to the throne of Naples over his rival monarch, King Joachim Murat. A year later on the 8th of March 1816, Ferdinand merged his two thrones of Sicily and Naples into one throne, thereby being known as the King of the Two Sicilies, a kingdom he continued to rule over until his death on the 4th of January 1825.

Ferdinand did in fact marry one of his sons, Leopoldo, to the Archduchess Clementina of Austria, just four years after this story took place in 1816, their marriage made to strengthen the ties between their two countries.

As usual, I do my very best to keep all elements of historical information as precise as possible, although the main characters I write about are always fictional, and as such so were Anteros and Olivia. Thank you all for joining me on their adventure across the high seas. It has been an absolute pleasure to write their story and to bring it to you.

Her Pirate Prince

~ COMING NEXT ~

Regency Brides Series, Book Six
(A Continuing Adventure for Anteros and Olivia)

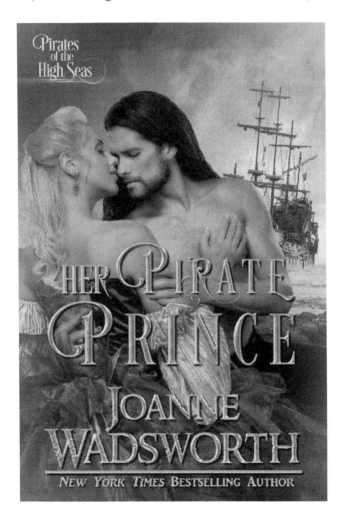

Regency Brides

The Duke's Bride, Book One
The Earl's Bride, Book Two
The Wartime Bride, Book Three
The Earl's Secret Bride, Book Four
The Prince's Bride, Book Five
Her Pirate Prince, Book Six
Chased by the Corsair, Book Seven

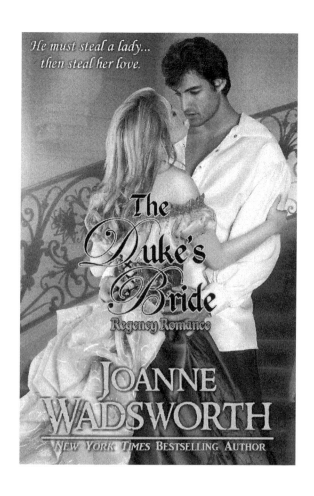

The Matheson Brothers

Highlander's Desire, Book One
Highlander's Passion, Book Two
Highlander's Seduction, Book Three

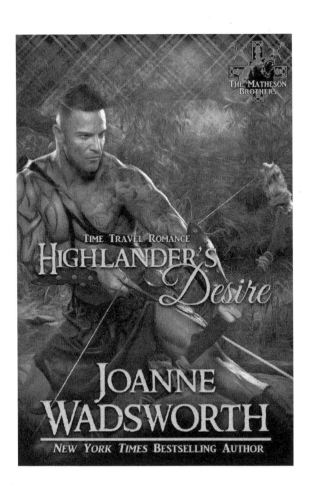

JOANNE WADSWORTH

The Matheson Brothers Continued

Highlander's Kiss, Book Four
Highlander's Heart, Book Five
Highlander's Sword, Book Six

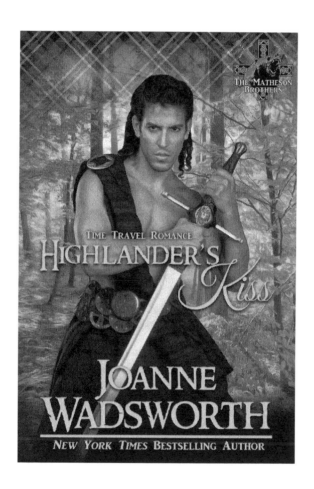

The Matheson Brothers Continued

Highlander's Bride, Book Seven
Highlander's Caress, Book Eight
Highlander's Touch, Book Nine

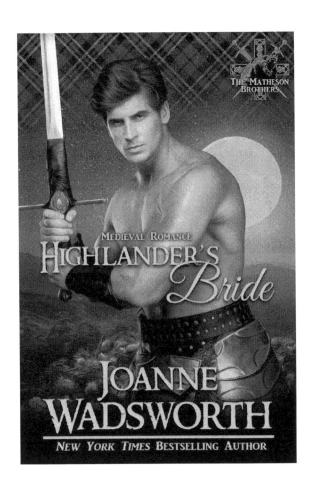

JOANNE WADSWORTH

The Matheson Brothers Continued

Highlander's Shifter, Book Ten
Highlander's Claim, Book Eleven
Highlander's Courage, Book Twelve
Highlander's Mermaid, Book Thirteen

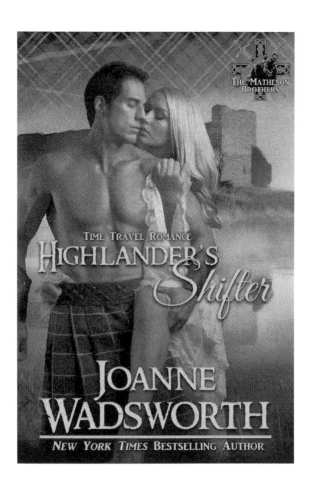

Highlander Heat

Highlander's Castle, Book One
Highlander's Magic, Book Two
Highlander's Charm, Book Three
Highlander's Guardian, Book Four
Highlander's Faerie, Book Five
Highlander's Champion, Book Six

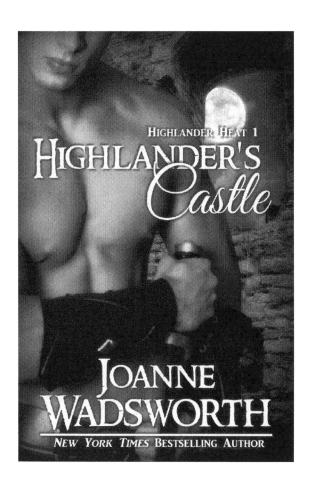

JOANNE WADSWORTH

Princesses of Myth

Protector, Book One
Warrior, Book Two
Hunter (Short Story - Included in Warrior, Book Two)
Enchanter, Book Three
Healer, Book Four
Chaser, Book Five

THE PRINCE'S BRIDE

Billionaire Bodyguards

Billionaire Bodyguard Attraction, Book One
Billionaire Bodyguard Boss, Book Two
Billionaire Bodyguard Fling, Book Three

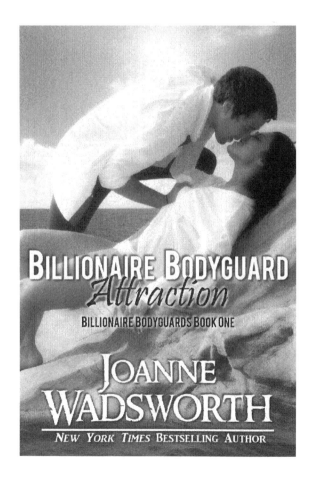

JOANNE WADSWORTH

Joanne Wadsworth is a *New York Times* and *USA Today* Bestselling Author who adores getting lost in the world of romance, no matter what era in time that might be. Hot alpha Highlanders hound her, demanding their stories are told and she's devoted to ensuring they meet their match, whether that be with a feisty lass from the present or far in the past.

Living on a tiny island at the bottom of the world, she calls New Zealand home. Big-dreamer, hoarder of chocolate, and addicted to juicy watermelons since the age of five, she chases after her four energetic children and has her own hunky hubby on the side.

So come and join in all the fun, because this kiwi girl promises to give you her "Hot-Highlander" oath, to bring you a heart-pounding, sexy adventure from the moment you turn the first page. This is where romance meets fantasy and adventure…

To learn more about Joanne and her works, visit
http://www.joannewadsworth.com

Made in the USA
Middletown, DE
06 November 2023